REPUBLIC OF NORTH LONDON

REPUBLIC OF NORTH LONDON
Barry Stewart Hunter

First published in 2023 by
Martin Firrell Company Ltd., Unit 4 City Limits,
Danehill, Reading RG6 4UP, United Kingdom

ISBN 978-1-912622-40-5

Typeset in Baskerville.

For Rob, Mike & Scott

CONTENTS

The Blood Diaries

'THAT DEXTER DOOLITTLE REGARDED himself as the unluckiest man in the world was probably the most singular thing about him.' And here, Nathan, having cleared his throat decisively, rises to his feet behind his desk and plants his desert boots wider apart before continuing in a lower, more confident register. 'True, the chap had a memorable name, a moniker both alien and familiar, a name he himself enjoyed for the very attention, not always flattering, it had attracted over time. Notable name aside, however, he exhibited few exceptional characteristics that might have found their way, by the grace of God and with a following wind, into the credit columns of the ledger of personal attributes. He was small and round, with a too red face. He was prone in an unfortunate degree to perspiration. His hair had parted company with the roof of his head quite suddenly, and at a remarkably tender age, this misfortune compounded in an unhappy twist of fate by the proliferation ever since, despite regular attempts to contain them, of unruly tufts in and around his nostrils and ears. As to his disposition – he was as stoical as a sheep or cow in the face of any and every reversal. "Oh, look," Dexter would say to himself excitedly. "The sun has got his hat on today!" And out he would rush, folding chair in hand, to the little garden at the back of his house in a modest village far from the nearest city, only to find

3

the sun had chosen to withdraw at short notice and with no obvious timetable for return. "Not to worry," Dexter would say. "The sun, that scheming charmer, will only make my face redder and my skin clammier." Disappointments of this nature were meat and drink to Dexter Doolittle. If he stepped off the pavement in order to avoid passing beneath the window cleaner's ladder you can be certain the postman's van, swerving at just that moment to dodge a lost puppy in the middle of the village high street, would send a shower of dirty rainwater in the direction of Dexter's burgundy corduroy trousers and blue suede shoes. "Never mind – one day the wind will change course, whereupon fortune will befriend me." That was all the poor fellow's mantra. As the years came and went, and life appeared to pass him by, he waited patiently for his luck to change –'

Nathan Ford, twenty-something postgraduate student reading English with options in creative writing, folds his typed sheets of A4 paper carefully and sits down at his desk under the practised eye at the lectern of Donald Donaldson, inspirational teacher, acclaimed author, concerned father, failed husband. Applause, generous and authentic for the most part, if driven by a soupçon of anxiety in the minds of those students who are yet to read, runs through the small classroom and out through an open sash window to reach eventually the furthest outposts of Queen Anne's, the internationally recognised seat of learning famed for its unbending devotion to the liberal arts and for its darling campus nestling contentedly – *smugly*, detractors and drop-outs might say – in a desirable enclave of the republic of north London. At this time of the morning the thoughts of students and teachers alike turn as often as not to an interdisciplinary picnic lunch under the old plane trees of the historic courtyard at the heart of the estate. Soon they will gather in this leafy quadrangle, laptops under their arms and smartphones to hand. It is early in June, that ravishing month when everything seems right with the world, and summer must be seized with both hands or else forfeited entire.

THERE IS A TERRACED HOUSE in Finsbury Park (or Highbury Barn, if you're out to impress), a nice house with four good-sized bedrooms and a south-facing garden having a decked area and a lawn about half the length of a cricket pitch. In this nice house live Donald and Tamara Donaldson – he a lecturer at a top university, she a lawyer specialising in immigration and human rights issues – and their two children, Henry (but not Harold or Harry) and Alice, aged fifteen and nine respectively. Whereas Henry enjoys painting by numbers without ever going over the line, and doing cryptic crossword puzzles (he used, during a difficult phase, to like playing with dolls, but that is another story), Alice often lists swimming underwater among her favourite things. In fact, Donaldson will take Alice swimming at Swiss Cottage tomorrow morning, it being Saturday there all day. He is currently teaching her how to plunge into the drink from the side of the pool (the diving platforms proper, if they ever open them, may feature later) without making a splash. For the father there is a vital life-lesson element to these poolside endeavours – a metaphorical fitness that is, thus far, lost on the daughter. The splash associated with every dive, although in many ways a postscript to the principal event, is crucial to a well-judged entry.

They are at supper in the second reception room. Tamara sits at one end of the table under a framed portrait of her done in mixed media with collage, wedding gift fifteen years ago of an impecunious artist cousin who lives in a different type of homestead not far away. Henry and Alice, seated opposite each other across the middle part of the vast table, glare down at the food getting steadily colder on their plates. This evening, as usual, the daughter will eat something

5

bland of her own choosing. The son, as befits his age and status, has the same meal as his parents most nights.

'Aren't you going to pour out your little glass of wine, Henry?' Tamara asks, breaking a long silence. 'I think we should just start, don't you?'

'Where *is* he?' the son says, as if enquiring after a runaway pet.

'Would you like to light the candles for Daddy, Alice, dear?'

'I'm not hungry, Mummy. Please can I leave the table?'

'Not yet, dear. Oh, Henry, darling – why don't you recite the Selkirk grace for us while we wait?'

'What's he *doing* up there, Mum? If it was me, he'd let me know all about it. And that's another thing. I'm old enough to drink *wine*, but I'm too young to ride my bike on the street. Is that it?'

'Please don't start all that again, darling. You know what your father thinks about it.'

At the top of the house, in a cleverly converted loft space, is the master bedroom with dinky little shower room attached. It is here in the shower room, his trousers and underpants around his ankles, that Donaldson masturbates at the white wash hand basin in front of a mirrored cabinet. He isn't thinking about his wife at this hour. He isn't thinking about anyone specific. Although he tries very hard to conjure up a sexual image, or – better – an image series, that will carry him over the line, the fact is he is struggling to bring the whole thing off successfully and in a timely fashion. That they are waiting for him at the supper table in the through reception room two floors below only adds to Donaldson's anxiety. It is the stark white basin that does for him every time. It actually hurts his eyes. Yet the sheer whiteness of the wash hand basin is central to his enquiries. He is looking for the blood. Is the blood still there? The white basin never lies, Donaldson tells himself again with a last look in the mirror.

6

At the table he apologises for his lateness, then asks Henry to say the Selkirk grace because he knows the boy loves to do it. He has always liked saying those strong, simple words attributed to Burns.

'We've already *done* that,' Henry says in a way that suggests the world, his world, has recently ended with a pathetic whimper. 'I'm not going to do it again just for you, if you don't mind –'

If Donaldson minds, he doesn't admit it. He would dearly love to ask his son to do it again, just for him, but he is reluctant to risk being rejected by a teenaged youth in his own house. Their supper is another largely unspeaking affair with the potential for emotional upheaval from one minute to the next. They are a nuclear family in a Bafta-nominated short film – at any time the troubled son might make a shattering personal declaration.

'We can't go on like this,' Tamara says after Alice and Henry have both left the table.

'Like what, exactly?' asks Donaldson, draining the wine bottle while managing to peer into his wife's eyes across distance. It occurs to him he doesn't actually know what colour her eyes are. Surely, he once knew. Perhaps he has simply forgotten over time. Her hair, which she used to wear long, is now shorter, but not too short, as if she is hedging her bets in the hair stakes. Short hair will come after. Although it is still light outside, the candles are lit. Without warning, the flicker of candlelight in his wife's eyes transports Donaldson to the restaurant in Paris where she told him she was pregnant for the first time. There are starched white tablecloths here in abundance. There are the stiff bibs of waiters, contemptuously white. Green – her eyes are greyish green in colour. Much like most people's eyes, Donaldson concludes for no obvious reason. 'What's on your mind, lovely?' he adds finally, shrugging his shoulders and then cocking his head while striving at all times to be in the moment.

'Maybe we should look at buying a second place,' Tamara says. 'Can we even afford that? A place in the country, or beside the sea. Somewhere far away from everyone.'

'As in far away from each other, perchance?'

'You said it – not me. I meant far away from everything. I just need some space, that's all.'

'Ah, yes, space –' Donaldson confirms, nodding with empathy behind his raised glass. 'The final frontier.'

IN AN UPSTAIRS SEMINAR ROOM AT Queen Anne's in Hampstead the applause for one reading drops off as expectation for the next outing starts to build. High pressure is drawing up warm air from Spanish Sahara, and the leaves of the tree at the first-floor window barely stir in the languid breeze.

'Way to travel, Nathan,' comments Donaldson enthusiastically from the front of the room. 'We'll look forward to discussing that opening paragraph, so full of Russian promise, just as soon as we've heard from one or two others here today.' Now the senior lecturer casts his eye over the class and smiles encouragingly for the benefit of eight further students, each one of them a budding Chekhov or Maupassant in the making, or so they dare to believe. Which one of them has what it takes to go the full distance? Which one of them is talented enough, or hungry enough, or lucky enough, or ruthless enough to eclipse all the others? To Donald Donaldson, supremely alone at the lectern and with a vital engagement in mind for later, these questions describe a roadmap to the past, to a time when he was happy and successful, the two conditions presenting themselves ideally and ironically side by side in the imagination of the writer and the man. 'So, who's next, boys and girls?' he enquires warmly, fondly even, of his current complement. What do they really know

8

of anything? Where is it to be found – that subtle and illuminating quality with which to do justice to the futility of existence? There is a wary silence inside the classroom at this point. There is little eye contact to be made with certain coy students at this time. Cue the rush of ambition to youthful hearts. And for Donaldson there is no relief. His daughter is a stranger to him, his son a provocation. Is his wife of fifteen years preparing to walk out on him? He wouldn't bet against that possibility. The blood – it is still there. That's right – the blood is still active in Donaldson's seminal fluid. And now he has the absurd idea his most promising student is taking the mickey out of him in the guise of a Russian master storyteller.

'OK – let's rewind here. The character in Nathan's piece, one Dexter Doolittle – what do we discover about him from the get-go, Melanie?'

'Well, Don – we learn he's uncommonly unlucky. Or, at least, he thinks he is.'

'You're right, Melanie. This individual seems to be cursed with various physical afflictions, quite apart from anything else. But does he mind or care?'

'I really don't think he does. Dexter appears to shrug off every misfortune with a cheerful stoicism.'

'So, we expect him to be one thing – angry, maybe, or resentful – but we discover he's actually something very different to that. And this surprises us, doesn't it? How about it, Siobhan?'

'It makes us feel sympathetic towards the character. It makes us warm to him. It also alerts us to the possibility that this story may not be about what we thought it was going to be about.'

'And what kind of story is it, I wonder? Any thoughts, Reuben?'

'We don't know yet. We haven't seen quite enough. To me this is a tale about an unlucky man who's waiting for his luck, and with it his life, to change. Beyond that, we can only speculate at this early stage in the proceedings.'

'Themes, Dylan – any contenders at this time?'

'I couldn't tell you. Unless this is going to be something about the pursuit of happiness. Is the pursuit of happiness a good or a bad thing? Is it, perhaps, a form of selfishness? Maybe we ought to give ourselves up to the idea that we should accept our fate gracefully or graciously and just get on with it.'

It is almost certainly time to bring Nathan himself back into the conversation. And, look – he is already on his feet, as if his presence here today is a matter of social responsibility, of good manners, say, or fine breeding. He is expertly made in a long-limbed kind of way, Donaldson notes objectively, as if laying the foundations for a short story starring Nathan Ford, that sexy left-hander. Now the redhead student toys with a cross around his neck and flashes the friendship bracelets at his wrist, these last picked up in the souk at Fez, perhaps, or a surf shack in Puerto Escondido on an annual road trip with his enlightened parents. They are youngish and carefree, these parents. This is how Donaldson invariably sees them – the whole lot of them, that is. They are all of independent spirit and means – at least in the imagination of the senior lecturer. They have recorded a Christmas novelty hit single, or sold an image of a goldfish in a bowl to IKEA, and now their talented sons and daughters are destined to scoop a Pulitzer or a Grammy or an Emmy or a Tony. These are privileged kids – smart, sensitive kids. That is why they are mostly named after Beat novelists and singer-songwriters from another time and place, a far better time and place. For every Melanie there is a Donovan or a Woody. As for this or that precocious Dylan – the key to reading these, according to Donaldson's theory of personality and potential, lies in choosing between a visionary Welsh poet with a King James bible and a rock star Nobel laureate with a Fender guitar. One more thing – if the postgraduate student now on his feet has a first-class body, how can he legitimately expect to be a great writer?

'Looks like you own the floor, Nathan. Does any of what you've heard strike a chord with you?'

'So, this is my lucky day, right? The truth is I had no idea what my story was about up until five or six minutes ago. But, hey – now I know exactly where I'm heading with this baby. I mean – fate and the pursuit of happiness? Count me in, guys. I'll take all I can get.'

The students laugh sincerely (it is too early in the semester for the daggers to come out), and it is tacitly agreed in the oak-panelled room today's session has been a success. Melanie reads a short piece about the death of Randall Jarrell, which gives Donaldson an idea for a future class, and then Dylan presents a scene from an endless screenplay in which his American namesake writes Sad Eyed Lady Of The Lowlands in the Chelsea Hotel, New York City, over the course of three hallucinatory days without sleep. Someone closes the sash window, but not before a fighter jet passes low overhead with a terrific roar on its way to RAF Lossiemouth or one of those places you hear about on the six o'clock news, and Donaldson has a vision of a sleek aircraft crashing and burning off the Norfolk coast as the pilot descends serenely below a canopy of Vietnamese silk.

'Do you mix socially with your students at all?' asks Siobhan from the shadow of the lectern as the class breaks for lunch.

'It has been known –' Donaldson says equably. 'But only in safe numbers and this side of midnight.'

'Cool – so, you're invited to my twenty-third birthday party a week tomorrow. It's a sixties do – I know how much you like themes. That's the *nineteen*-sixties, in case you're wondering. And please feel free to bring a friend. Or even just your wife.'

11

HE IS ACCELERATING AND BRAKING, stopping and then starting. He has taken the Northern line via Camden Town, changing later for Finsbury Park and home, and now he is in the ancient Renault on the North Circular Road heading east. All three lanes are chocker. He is on schedule at this point, but all that can change in the blink of an eye on the crummy superhighway from here to nowhere.

There is a white van in Donaldson's rear-view mirror. A white van man is tailgating the Renault aggressively. When the man pulls out abruptly to overtake, Donaldson catches a glimpse of a ruddy maniac behind the wheel, his middle finger raised in salute. There is a ritual honking of horns here, but Donaldson isn't listening. He is thinking about the ruddy face of a maniac and how it puts him in mind of Nathan Ford's story. Now Donaldson struggles to recall the details of the story. There is the too red face and the bald head and the hairy ears and the clammy skin. No, he is nothing like Nathan's protagonist. He is nothing like him at all. Then it comes, or comes back, to Donaldson with a little jolt. It is in the juxtaposition of the names. Dexter Doolittle and Donald Donaldson – all the Ds are on parade. Is the senior lecturer acting reasonably in proposing such a link? Why would his most promising student choose to make fun of him in the first place? Why should it matter if he did? Although on any other day of the week it wouldn't matter, somehow today it does. What does all that signify or amount to? It marks a shift in relations, surely. It means someone's life is set to change. How else to read the thing? As he swings the car into the piddling little car park at North Middlesex University Training Hospital Donaldson's heart misses a beat. Heading directly towards him in a no-nonsense manner is his new friend in the white van. Is it he? How could it be otherwise? A couple of things preoccupy Donaldson at more or less the same time. First, he has no plans to surrender that last parking space to anyone under any circumstances. Securing that lovely space – it is strictly a matter of life and death, Donaldson concludes. There is also his growing awareness of the shoe issue. Does he or does he not possess a pair of blue suede shoes of the kind referenced in Nathan's story? With regard to the famous burgundy trousers the senior lecturer is quietly confident of his innocence. (Can he be confident of anything in the current psychological climate? If such corduroy trousers exist, they must be exiled immediately to a realm beyond the reach of the most fertile imagination.) Ah, but those sad shoes – Donaldson has always known they would conspire to bring him low one day. And now that day has arrived.

He surrenders the golden parking space. Naturally, he does. It takes him three and a half minutes to locate another space and pay for it, and when he reaches the entrance to the monstrous palace of healing he discovers his new friend is waiting there to offer up some words of advice.

'You want to watch yourself in these parts.'

'Really?' Donaldson says, feeling wretched and shaken, but also honest and true.

'This ain't exactly your manor, unless I'm much mistaken.'

'You're very perceptive – I see that now. But you stole my space – I hope you understand that.'

'And I hope you understand I could break your legs.'

'Oh, please – do me a favour. Now, if you don't mind – I'm late for my appointment.'

'We're all late for our fucking appointment,' snarls the man, and there is an aphoristic-cum-philosophical quality to this outburst that cheers Donaldson momentarily as he passes through the automatic doors of the hospital. We are all connected to each other at a basic level, he tells himself. White van man is really just a version of me.

'Try to be kinder to yourself,' he calls out from the mat as the sliding doors stutter on either side of him. 'You might actually find some of it rubs off on other people.'

One hour later he is back in the now half-empty car park. His hunch of fifty-six minutes' duration is wide of the mark. The faithful Renault is unchanged. None of its tyres has been slashed.

I DON'T THINK DAD REALLY loves me. I mean – I think he struggles with that calling. I sometimes think he sees me as a disappointment compared to his clever writing students. He once gave me a Conrad novel for my birthday and took great satisfaction in advising me I wouldn't find any boy wizards in its pages. When he asked me later what I thought of the book I told him it was good. When he asked me in what way or ways, I said in every way. I think he knew I never finished that novel, but he didn't want to countenance the lie. Truth is a big deal with my father. I think part of the thing with his Conrad birthday gift lay elsewhere – he wanted me to be more of a man. I don't know how to help him with that.

The first indication I had that something might be wrong with Dad came when I was vacuuming the car. Once a month I get paid twenty quid in pocket money to clean the Renault inside and out. There were two parking charge slips – the kind you peel and stick to your windscreen – on the mat below the pedals with the name of a hospital somewhere in the north of the city. One such parking slip you could ignore – Dad might have been visiting a sick student or colleague (it wouldn't have been the first time). But two slips made the whole thing different. Mum refuses to drive that car, which she calls a death trap. It's true Dad could have driven *her* to the hospital, but that wasn't the sense I got. It was right after cleaning the Renault that I decided to do a little detective work.

14

I already knew Dad's password for his computer – a huge Apple affair whose inexorable obsolescence was a source of pride to him. The password was Password1 deployed backwards, this backwards business being a further source of satisfaction. Of course, in sharing his password with me, Dad was sending me an important message. I guess trust is second only to truth with him. I remember he once told me I'd have to become head of the family one day. That's what the password thing was all about.

I'm not sure what I expected to find on the desktop. There were about twenty folders related to teaching and writing – notes about classes and fragments of fiction, mostly. I knew Dad kept a diary, which he called a journal – he said he turned to his journal when he was stuck for story ideas. As far as I knew, Dad hadn't written a story in years. Even so, I didn't have to work too hard or dig too deep. I didn't find the journal as such, but I found something else – the only loose file on the desktop, labelled TBD.

To whom it may concern – in accessing my father's computer without his knowledge or permission I know I was doing wrong, and I hereby invite you to design a suitable punishment for what I did.

When he met with the blood, Dad decided to sit on the whole thing. In other words, he did nothing about it. Immediately, I got to thinking about how he might have discovered it in the first place. It must be hard having someone else point it out, after all. I began to hope that Dad had discovered the blood off his own bat. I don't even know if they have sex any more up there in the master bedroom. I certainly haven't heard evidence of it recently, although I used to – nothing in the way of expressive commentary, of course, but rather a low-key mechanical straining of parts.

After six weeks (the maximum delay prescribed by the internet), Dad finally saw a GP who asked him about his sexual history and a bunch of other stuff to do with a familial predisposition to cancer. That's how it began. They took enough blood for a barrage of tests, and told Dad to await further instructions. I could see the date the computer file had been started. I even thought I knew what the label TBD stood for. Dad was keeping a diary dedicated to the blood. He probably thought it would provide the basis for a story one day (he saw pretty much everything, good and bad, in those terms). Dad's diary was written in a light-hearted way – with irony, he would have said. And now his diary will be a part of mine. I have never felt as close to Dad as I do today, writing about the blood – his blood. But he will never find that out – not as things stand. How can I discuss with him what I'm not supposed to know?

What else? There is a clinic in Belsize Park that supports young people looking to transition. I hate my body. My body disgusts me today. But will it disgust me any less tomorrow? I mean *after*? There is a third way, of course. I call this the nuclear option, or the ultimate self-harm. Yes, there is a third way, provided I have the strength to go through with the thing. What is strength anyway? Being strong has nothing to do with *strength* strength, it seems to me. Rather, it has everything to do with existing – no, surviving – in a world that wasn't made for me to be in it. (Thank you, God, for that last bit.) And there is only so much strength. Courage will run down. What's to do? In the end there is not enough heart to go round.

PART TWO

All the Moves

IN THE RUN-UP TO SIOBHAN'S birthday party Donaldson makes an assumption. Calculating that his wife will hate the idea of attending a student do (she normally runs a mile from his university activities, official or otherwise), he fails to mention the party invitation. On the evening in question, however, he winds up interrogating the ethical logic of his approach. As he confronts the frankly ludicrous prospect of having to gift-wrap his Penguin edition, battered but original, of The L-Shaped Room *in secret*, he comes to a settled view based on a natural feeling for justice. It is only right that Tamara be given the opportunity to turn down tonight's invitation in her own words and her own way. Does she need space? Let there be space in her outlook with immediate effect. It is a little after six on Saturday, and she has already had her first gin and tonic of the evening.

'A sixties theme?' she exclaims with exaggerated delight. 'But how perfectly and retrospectively charming. I shall dust off my flared trouser suit and you can dig out your kaftan.'

'There probably isn't time,' says Donaldson, wrongfooted but adjusting fast to his wife's unscheduled enthusiasm, 'to insert garish triangular patches into the legs of my jeans tonight.'

'Now, there's a happy thought,' Tamara says, thinking. 'You were never very good at fancy dress, were you, darling? Not to worry

– hopefully there's going to be some superior marijuana doing the rounds. I think that's the least one might expect of all your wannabe Woolfs and fledgling Forsters.'

'These are *young* people,' Donaldson reminds her. 'They intend to live long and prosper.'

'What became of live fast, die young?' she asks. 'No, don't tell me – a failed social experiment. And so last century. Are we likely to meet any parents there, do you think?'

'We can take the car,' he says with a fresh focus on the practical. She is already tipsy. He senses danger. Why are they talking like two people who have recently met, unless it is because they are shortly to part? 'I said I'd stick my head in for an hour or so just to show my face. Apparently, there's finger food –'

'I do love a buffet,' she says, drawing her hair into the makings of a pony tail and then releasing it. 'We're not taking the bloody *car*,' she adds, snatching a phone from the kitchen table. 'We really don't want to end up being towed off the road, now, do we? Luckily, we have digital options. So, where is this youthful debauch, anyway?'

First, they tell Henry they'll be back by eleven. Then they ask him to read a story to Alice. This is in the main reception room, an elegant but comfortable space endowed with period features, where brother and sister observe separate screens, headphones lowered in a temporary concession to something.

'She hates it when I read to her,' Henry says without rancour. 'Tell them, Alice.'

'He goes too quickly,' Alice complains. 'And he doesn't do the voices properly.'

An hour and a half later they draw up in an immaculate Uber at an address off Camden Square, NW1. Donaldson gives his wife the gift-wrapped paperback to present when the moment arrives, but she hands it straight back. The party is set across three floors of the building and takes in as many separate flats, plus the staircases and landings that connect them. The downside to this democratic arrangement is that it is hard to get one's bearings at any given time and still harder to locate the host.

'Siobhan? You'll find her in the middle flat – so much easier to segue upwards or downwards from there.'

The middle flat, a tasteful repository of rattan furniture, feature wallpaper and exotic botanicals, turns out to be the administrative hub of tonight's enterprise. Below it lies the music and dance zone. Tamara has already reconnoitred this lower-level space with an eye, or an ear, on what she describes – to Donaldson's mild horror – as *a quick bop sometime later.*

'Do you actually live here?' Donaldson asks Siobhan, having tracked her down to the kitchen of the middle flat where she is busy halving Scotch eggs.

'No way,' she says, pulling a face. 'These stuccoed cliffs are far too expensive for little old *moi.* I'm really just piggy-backing tonight on two other complementary soirées.'

'Of course,' Donaldson confirms dubiously. 'So, what happens upstairs?' He is genuinely curious here – he hasn't been to a student party on this scale since he was a student.

'Upstairs is the chill-out area,' Siobhan explains in the patient tone of a kindergarten teacher.

'Great,' Donaldson says, nodding his approval. 'Here – I got you this. As a matter of fact, my wife chose it – she has much better taste in literature than me.'

'Ha, ha – are you trying to tell me it's a book?'

A short time later they hover in a huddle in the living room of the flat, human traffic coming and going around them. Donaldson and Tamara sip red and white wine respectively. Siobhan, who is pacing herself, nurses a small spritzer. Donaldson gives up trying to explain to himself why he said what he said about the book. He is on the point of reaching out to Melanie, who forms part of a nearby conversational pod, when his wife distracts him excitedly.

'Oh, my God – look at that. Is that what I think it is?' Tamara points to the big bay window where a barefoot young woman with long wavy hair sits on the ledge beside a cat. 'Is that supposed to be the album cover picture for Tapestry?' Tamara asks incredulously. 'But wasn't that the seventies?'

Later, chatting to Melanie in the shadow of a triumphant palm, Donaldson works flat out to define or divine the significance of the party in personal or political terms. There must be a reason why he is here tonight, a reason other than the obvious one that has to do with having been invited. He is on the threshold of something – but what is it? Is it something good or something bad? This notion he has of impending change, of shipwreck imminent and inevitable, is back in spades. A sweat breaks out inside Donaldson's shirt. Is he right to believe it – this sense he has that his life is set to crash down around him? His every action or choice matters utterly in the face of such hostile intentions, he decides, suppressing a funk he hardly recognises. And they are all implicated. His wife, son and daughter – even his students – they are all part of it, whatever *it* is. He is in a dogfight. He must be ready for anything, Donaldson tells himself, rallying at the last. Then he remembers the blood.

'But do you think it's a fit topic at the end of the day?' Melanie asks, touching his hand – the one holding his glass – intimately while he struggles to stay on subject and on message.

'The death of Randall Jarrell? Absolutely – why not? The idea that he walked out in front of that car deliberately is something that haunts me. I think it haunts all serious writers. Do you know what? It puts me in mind of what happened to JG Farrell. Do you know Farrell's work? If not, you should definitely get acquainted with it. Very good on Ireland and empire. Anyway, Farrell died in a strange drowning accident off the Irish coast. But the idea was put about that he wanted to drown. He was ambivalent about being rescued, according to an eye witness who tried to help him. In other words, he wasn't sure about being saved.'

'Oh, my gosh – that's totally freaky,' Melanie says, draining her wine glass and casting around for a source of fresh supply. 'Maybe I could link those two stories. What do you think, Don? I mean – their names actually *rhyme*, right? Jarrell and Farrell –'

'Or perhaps find a third element – odd numbers always work best, don't they?'

'You're right. You're so right about that. Do you mind if I say something, Don?'

Later still, after he has deflected Melanie's harmless advances with a practised hand, he enters the lower-level apartment in search of his wife. Here, as in the flat above, the sixties spill randomly into the seventies to create a hybrid soundtrack pleasing to all. There is a circle of grooving, clapping young people in the room with, at its centre, the couple of the hour. Yes, Tamara and Nathan Ford are experiencing an attack of Saturday night fever all their own to the widespread approval of those who look on. And Donaldson has to admit it. His student – his mickey-taking, Russian-riffing, short story specialist – has all the moves. No doubt a home truth is in play here, everyone agrees. Because he looks good, Nathan dances well.

'Are you trying to embarrass all of us, both of us, or just me?' he asks Tamara in the cab, this enquiry designed to reveal what his wife of fifteen years really thinks of him on a night of mixed signals.

'Fuck off –' she says, a little breathlessly. 'He actually told me I was hot. As in H-O-T.'

HE IS IN A SCRAP – THAT IS WHAT it all means. Seconds out – round two. Is that the ping of a typewriter clattering away in a forgotten room? Or is it a bell inside his head? As he sits beside Tamara in a local silence outside the head teacher's office, Donaldson takes stock for the umpteenth time. Is she capable of having an affair? That idea is what is foremost in the husband's mind at this hour. And now it seems unbelievable that the matter is only just arising. Why today? Why this week? Is it possible his wife has conducted multiple affairs across the years and right under his nose without these ever coming to his attention? Why not ask her? Why not just pop the question, or questions? Isn't that what she would do in his shoes – in his blue suede shoes? He is within a whisker of moving this whole fascinating debate forward conclusively when a half-glass door opens without warning beside and slightly behind him.

'So sorry to keep you waiting,' says someone, a secretary type of person. 'Won't be long now –'

He can hear the voice of the head teacher soft and low on the blower from the other side of the wall. They have been summoned to a pow-wow at Henry's school, an expensive number in Highgate where he is a day pupil among boarders, the sons of barristers and bankers and consuls general. To Donaldson there is something quite poignant about what is happening here today. Are they penitents, the husband and the wife? They are like penitents sitting quietly on these plain wooden chairs in this scrubbed corridor. It occurs again to Donaldson he hasn't had sex – blood or no blood – with his wife for many months. The exact tally is difficult to pin down. She hasn't mentioned it at all. She hasn't drawn attention to it in any way. Of course, sex isn't everything. But what other compensating factors can he cite? He has written some books. Do they count for anything? Has his wife even read them? Donaldson can't be categorical there. He has a job, but then so does she. Is she conventional enough to want to stay together in the interests of the children only? She needs space, or so she says. Space to do what, though? To fuck Nathan, of course. What if she merely finds him – Donald Donaldson, author and educator – supremely dull? How to kindle a spark in her? Does he even want to do that? The realisation that he doesn't altogether care whether his wife of a decade and a half stays or goes prompts Donaldson to cry out involuntarily at a private school in N6.

'What's the matter, darling?' Tamara enquires in a voice that suggests she already knows.

'I was just thinking,' he says with a little laugh, 'about the first time we went to Paris together. I wanted to stay in bed with the do not disturb sign on the door. You wanted to go to Père Lachaise to see Jim Morrison's grave – again.'

In the head teacher's office, two occasional chairs are already positioned on this side of the desk and angled slightly towards each other. That's it, Donaldson thinks. We are not penitents. We are an ordinary couple at the offices of the marriage guidance counsellor. But where is that secretarial person? She is so discreet they haven't even heard her exit the room.

'Thank you both for coming at such short notice,' says the head teacher, a middle-aged man of natural authority and empathy, with a kind of weary brightness directed at each of his visitors in turn. 'I know we're all terribly busy, so let me get straight to the point. I'm rather concerned about young Henry. It seems to some of us who take these things very seriously that the boy is being bullied. I mean bullied in a physical way. As to the rest one can only guess –'

There is a gap here in the narrative. The head teacher, a man of fine judgement, waits for what he has said to take hold across the desk as Tamara and Donaldson regard each other blankly.

'Have you spoken to him?' Donaldson asks, shifting awkwardly in his chair.

'Of course,' the head teacher says. 'But I was intent on asking you the same question.'

The husband and the wife exchange further glances and shake their heads in concert.

'We haven't noticed anything unusual or untoward,' Tamara says, jumping ahead a question or two. 'What did he tell you?'

'Nothing,' the head teacher says. 'I mean he told me everything was fine. But I don't know that I believe him. Henry is a very serious young man, and I like him. Which is to say I am generally disposed to take him at his word. But not in this particular case.'

'What happened?' Donaldson says. 'Did something happen to our son?'

'I don't know,' the head teacher says. 'At least, I can't be sure. It's largely a feeling I have, based on many years in the saddle. Last week, Henry distinguished himself on the cricket field. He made a lot of runs and took a great many wickets against a visiting school. Half an hour after I watched him being carried shoulder high from the pitch by his team mates, I discovered him crying in the pavilion. I had gone there to congratulate him, but I actually found him in some distress. Now, it could be he had a headache or a toothache. Perhaps he felt unexpectedly moved by a sonnet dissected earlier in class. What do you think? Would a young man who has triumphed on the field of battle just half an hour ago *cry*? This is not right, and I urge you to take the matter up with Henry immediately. What I haven't said yet is this. When I came across your son, he was naked and dripping wet. I should tell you that there are no showers in the cricket pavilion I refer to. I hardly need add that we remain alert at all times to our safeguarding responsibilities here at the school.'

They get as far as the tube station before she bursts into tears. 'Bastards,' she says. 'What have they done to him?'

'It's OK,' Donaldson says soothingly. 'We'll get to the bottom of it tonight. Do you want to speak to him? You know he likes you more than he likes me.'

'Don't be so bloody ridiculous, Don,' she says, sniffing. 'You're his father, for Christ's sake.'

She is correct on all counts. He is Henry's father and he is also ridiculous – ridiculous to himself, which is far from ideal. It is this feeling he has that the boy will reject him if he tries to get close, or closer, which unnerves him. His son is in distress – that is the main thing to remember. But it wouldn't do to get too close to him, would it, at his age? How close is too close? Is there a measuring stick or a set of scales? All this is normal, Donaldson assures himself. All this is normal between a father and son at a certain point in their secret, unknowable lives. And today that point has been reached.

'Will you be all right?' he asks Tamara as their train rattles into Camden Town station.

'Of course,' she says. 'I have to get back to court. So, are you changing here for Queen Anne's?'

'I am,' he tells her, although he is not being entirely sincere. He is changing here, yes, but his ultimate destination is not the darling campus with its hallowed courtyard and monumental plane trees.

IT IS AS IT ALWAYS IS. ON THE NORTH Circular Road the traffic is diabolical. And to Donaldson it is like a recurring dream or, rather, a nightmare. He is being followed. He is being pursued by a flotilla, scattered randomly across three lanes, of white vans of many engine sizes and marques, having all of them behind the wheel a red-faced maniac. When he reaches the hospital car park he is duly surprised to find it half-full or half-empty. Now his dreamscape collapses. Of his ruddy friend there is no suggestion.

First, they ask him to sign a form in case his heart gives up the ghost mid-procedure. Then they ask him to take off his clothes and lie on a bench covered with a plastic sheet. There are three of them today – a main man who will lead the session, a female intern with a clipboard, and another gentleman whose role has something to do with standards. After the main man has rubbed an anaesthetic balm into the tip of the patient's penis, the camera is inserted, and off they go. Donaldson is invited to observe the inside wall of his bladder on a screen above his head while the probe reports back as if from the red planet or the Mariana trench.

He is not thinking about his bladder. He is not thinking about his son – that must come after, in due course. In fact, he is thinking about his wife of fifteen years – again. Only, this time the picture is different – more nuanced, maybe. Donaldson doesn't hate his wife. Naturally, he doesn't. That he no longer loves her is something else entirely. There is no shame in this. Of course, there isn't. It is life and life only. A little earlier today his wife's maternal instincts were magnificently aroused in respect of her teenaged son. Donaldson really admires that. He loves that. But as the bladder probe fails to discover anything inside him, the question returns to nag the man lying on a padded bench. Is his wife fucking Nathan Ford? She has only just met him, yes, but are they *doing* it? Is it possible they have known each other for some time – several semesters, say? In which case, they might have been banging away for months right under Donaldson's nose. Where, though? At the student's house? No, too

26

risky by half. Where, then? On neutral territory, of course. There is a hotel in central London, a perfectly ordinary hotel popular with tourists who drag their lives behind them on little wheels. It is here in a nondescript room three storeys above Tottenham Court Road that the deed takes place, not too often, but just often enough. And to Donaldson peering up at a screen there is something quite fitting suddenly in these dangerous liaisons. That's it – they are not unlike Mrs Robinson and the graduate, our two lovebirds. This is how the husband views it. There is only one thing needed to confirm it. This very night his wife will reveal she plans to stay over with a girlfriend, or with her artist cousin Jamie, perhaps, in the near future. In the very near future. Yes, tonight is the night.

'All done,' says the main man cheerfully. 'You'll hear from the urologist shortly.'

'Did you locate any nasties?' Donaldson asks conversationally over his shoulder, zipping himself up.

'Not today, no. As I say, you'll be getting a follow-up letter from us very soon.'

Now the hospital car park is completely full. Wait – there is a white van circling and circling like a shark as Donaldson proceeds calmly towards a defenceless Renault. He is not afraid of white van man – that would be silly. White van man is simply an extension of him. Oh, my word – there is something different about the Renault. To Donaldson it looks changed. Is that because its rear windscreen has been shattered? Has a large bird fallen from the sky on top of the faithful jalopy? It is just about possible, Donaldson admits. Yet there is no albatross corpse to be found anywhere. The car is sound. Now the dreamscape takes on a revised aspect. We are in a pay and display car park in north London. In a corner of this desolate realm a man with a crowbar attacks a saloon car with terrific violence.

27

At the supper table that evening Henry says the Selkirk grace with extra feeling.

'When can I say it, Mummy?' Alice asks as she lights a candle.

'You don't even know what it means,' Henry says pleasantly.

'Yes, I do. It means thank you, God, for the nice chicken legs.'

'For the nice nuggets, you mean. And the spaghetti hoops.'

'Darling, please say you'll teach your little sister the words.'

'Why can't she teach herself? That's what I had to do, isn't it?'

'Be nice to Alice, Henry,' Donaldson says when he is alone at the table with his son. It is as agreed – Tamara has withdrawn with the younger child as early as possible. 'You were that age once.'

'I'm sorry. Is there something you wanted to say to me? I mean something else?'

'What gives you that idea?'

'I don't know. Is there, Dad?'

'I want you to tell me what happened to you in the pavilion at school last week.'

'Have you been talking to Mr Bennett?'

'Yes. But I'm not Mr Bennett. Please tell me what happened to you in the cricket pavilion.'

'Nothing happened to me. Someone emptied a bottle of water over me like it was champagne or something. I scored some runs and took some wickets – that's all.'

'You wouldn't lie to me, would you, Henry?' He is on the rocks at the margin of the water. To one side and slightly behind him are the deck chairs and the Martini parasols. This is somewhere in the south of France. His father is in the water a few yards further out where the tidal surges are less pronounced. The sea is coming and going every six seconds or so, coming and going. Donaldson must time his dive so that the water has reached its zenith as he enters it.

28

Then he will be sucked safely away from the rocks by the water as it recedes. There must be no splash, or very little, as he enters the water. A large seabird passes noiselessly from left to right. All this is perfectly clear to Donaldson. It is as if it happened yesterday, or the day before that. 'Are you all right, son? Is everything all right?'

The boy, a seasoned diver in the family tradition, says nothing. He doesn't nod or shake his head or anything. After a moment he asks to be excused and gets down from the table. Donaldson hears him sprint upstairs to his room.

In bed beside his wife, he turns it all over in his head. The sea water comes in and goes out with a slurping or slapping sound that is difficult to forget. He was never close to his own father, and he still doesn't know whose fault that is, or was.

'Maybe you should talk to him,' he says at last. 'I think there's something I can't get past with Henry.'

'Fine —' Tamara says. 'Leave it with me. But if he doesn't want to talk about it, we can't force him. Oh, and darling? I think I'll stay over at cousin Jamie's on Thursday night, if that's all right. He wants me to help him with his will, of all things. A thousand paintings in a cupboard, and no money in the bank.'

DAD HAS HAD A FLEXIBLE cystoscopy – an examination of urethra and bladder using a tiny camera on a long stalk. He doesn't say very much about it. I guess they didn't find anything alarming because no one got particularly worked up during the procedure. This latest diary entry concludes, as they all do to date, with three words – *blood still there.* And it strikes me I am looking ahead, as in looking forward, to the entry that says *no more blood*, or something along those lines. No doubt Dad will find a suitably humorous – no, ironic – way to capture the joyous moment. But what if that moment never comes?

What if all this marks the beginning of the end for Dad? Is this what he had in mind when he said I would have to become head of the family one day? Has he been dying slowly for years without telling anyone? It's a pity he feels he has no one to talk to about this whole rigmarole. He could always talk to me.

These twin possibilities – of blood and no blood – continue to drive me towards Dad's desktop. I have to ration my visits because it's actually a pretty negative experience to be inside someone else's computer without their say-so. Footsteps on the stairs – that's what you hear at any given moment. I wouldn't recommend it unless you happen to be the voyeuristic type. Scrolling back through the diary entries for June, I can see that Dad has had an ultrasound scan of testes and scrotum in addition to the business with the tiny camera. All they found was a testicular cyst, which they decided to ignore in the hunt for bigger fish. *Blood still there*. There is the portrait in words of Dad's urologist. Actually, this is more of a sketch in note form – racial type, accent, facial features, hair, hands, sense of humour (if any), and so on. The urologist it is who informs Dad his PSA value is normal for his time of life (when I search PSA on Dad's computer I find he has saved the web pages to his reading list in Safari). This urologist is the ultimate luck machine, the man who gets to insert a finger into Dad's rectum in order to assess the organ that is central to their investigations. Dad calls this shy orb either the kumquat or the quisling according to the politics of his mood and disposition.

I want to say something here about the cricket pavilion episode that has been exercising minds at home and abroad. For the record, I was assaulted in the cricket pavilion (specifically the squalid toilet) by three team mates – Jarvis (good with the bat), Ogilvie (handy with the ball), and Marshall (safe pair of hands on the boundary). I had made my half-century and taken five for twenty-seven – not bad for a girl in a boy's body – and they carried me from the field on their shoulders at stumps. In the toilet they clawed at my kit (I removed it myself in the end to prevent excess damage), later suspending me upside down with my head in the bowl before they pulled the chain. They flushed the toilet five times – once for each of those expensive wickets. To wait for the cistern to fill up in these circumstances is to break through from one level of consciousness to another. In many ways I am a changed person today, and I thank my team mates for that. Meanwhile, I have gone right off cricket both as a game and an ideal. All that metaphor-for-living guff – you can go tell it on the mountain. You may be asking why I haven't turned my team mates in. This is something I ask myself every day. It's a complex question that has to do with everything under the sun. If and when I find the answer, you'll be the second to know.

One more thing. I have investigated the famous clinic located in deepest Belsize Park, a stone's throw from where Freud himself lived during his sojourn in London. (To my mind this topographical equivalence is a good omen.) These are serious people. I feel certain they will take me seriously. I have begun to record my feelings and findings about transitioning in minute detail – just as Freud would have done. I imagine they will press me hard on every facet of my motivation or intent. They will try to catch me out, for that is their day job. I must be ready for anything, and I will be – cross my heart and hope to die. These indicators of desire – my every longing and yearning – I intend to commit to a separate diary. No, to a separate *journal* – a special journal, shot through very lightly with irony, of the kind Dad might keep. Always assuming, that is, I last that long –

Note to self – important to maintain a semblance of normality and continuity here, even though *the end*, according to the rules of the Sandie Shaw Fan Club (SSFC), is very much in sight now.

THE VERDICT IS IN. IT IS AS HE IMAGINED. Tamara will be doing it with Nathan Ford on Thursday night in a perfectly ordinary hotel bedroom in Tottenham Court Road, or nearest offer. She might as well have blurted it out in her sleep. She is guilty as charged. And now the object of her affection, or attention, is preparing to address the class in an oak-panelled seminar room above a leafy courtyard. They have been discussing Maupassant and Chekhov, short story pioneers with whom Donaldson, distracted here by any number of side issues, is mildly and professionally obsessed.

'To me, it's simple,' Nathan declares. 'The Frenchman likes to gratify you with a clever ending – a twist ending, if you will. But the Russian will have none of that. Often, there's no sense of an ending.'

Pretty good, Donaldson thinks. This student is pretty good at lots of things, including dancing and bedding other people's wives in hotels. 'That's good, Nathan,' says the senior lecturer, shrugging off for now the lingering sense he has that a certain Dexter Doolittle is modelled on him. 'I like that. Any other thoughts, anyone, on the difference between these two giants of the short form?'

'Maupassant,' ventures Melanie, 'wants to wrap everything up neatly.' If her eyes don't quite meet his eyes these days, it is because, Donaldson recognises, she went a bit too far at a recent party. 'You get the feeling he wants to tie his story up with a ribbon and bow.'

'Whereas Chekhov,' Siobhan adds, 'likes to keep you hanging on the telephone.'

'We might think of it this way,' Donaldson says, pacing. 'With Maupassant we've just finished an excellent dinner in the company of good friends. Now our host pushes his plate away and announces he's going to tell us a story. And when we reach the end of the tale, we find we enjoy the same satisfaction we got from our dinner. We are replete, in story terms. We have had just enough, and never too much. But with Chekhov we are looking at a river flowing past in front of us – the river of life, you might call it. And now the writer sticks one hand in the water here and the other hand in the water there, and in between lies our story. But the river carries on flowing on either side of these hands.'

'You could view that,' Reuben says, 'as a slice of life.'

'I'm not sure it's as clear cut as that,' Dylan says. 'Maupassant is perfectly happy to leave us up in the air, just as Chekhov is ready to wrap things up neatly when it suits him.'

'OK – thank you kindly,' Donaldson says. 'Now I want to try something completely different.' He is struggling mightily. He is not himself. His work-life balance is shot to pieces. Equilibrium is out of reach. He worries about his son. There is a wall between them. In Donaldson's imagination this wall rises inexorably towards heaven. How to smash the wall? He must open his heart. That's it – he must make himself vulnerable to the boy. He already *feels* vulnerable, but why doesn't it show? If it shows in his stories, why not in life? And there is something else. Yesterday he found himself unable to care very much whether his wife stayed or walked away. Why should he mind or care today if she is at it with one of his students? 'So, whose laptop can I commandeer for a few minutes?'

After he locates a recording of Gram Parsons doing Streets Of Baltimore he plays it to the class and informs them their next task is to retell the song's story from the woman's point of view. 'Make it sad, by all means,' he says. 'But make it true, please.'

'It's a country song, right?' Nathan says. 'All the pain of living is right there in those songs.'

One hour later Donaldson is in his office eating a salmon and cream cheese sandwich when, after barely knocking, Nathan pokes his head around the door and asks if he can come in.

'Am I disturbing you? I mean – can I talk to you for a minute?'

'Draw up a chair,' Donaldson says. 'I'll lunch while you talk.'

'I wanted to ask what you made of my story. The latest pages, I mean.'

'Dexter Doolittle?'

'Did you get it? Did you make the connection with the names? I guess it's glaringly obvious, right? My tale is a homage to you, the best teacher a boy could have.'

'A homage to me? That's extremely flattering. I haven't read the latest instalment yet, but I plan to.'

'Can I ask you something, Don? Is it OK if I call you Don? I know Melanie always calls you Don.'

'Is that what you wanted to ask me? If you can call me Don?'

'Not exactly. I wanted to ask if you'd care to have a drink with me sometime.'

Ah, yes. This is something different, Donaldson thinks. This is something other. And still there is no coy reference to dancing. Still there is no sheepish mention of his wife. 'Sure –' he says carefully. 'Just as long as we don't have to talk about your story all night long. I presume you're thinking about evening rather than lunchtime.'

'How about this Thursday after school?'

'Thursday?' says Donaldson, a light sweat breaking out under his arms. 'Are you quite sure you don't already have a date for this Thursday?' He only just remembers to omit it – the *with my wife* bit.

'Sure, I'm sure,' says the student, laughing. 'Why would I invite you otherwise? Oh, and you might want to wear a plaid shirt –'

Later, he stands at the window of his office and gazes down at the bike racks in the courtyard. Is it a trick, this latest development? Is it a trap, or a kind of twist ending? The more Donaldson berates himself, the more his scepticism takes hold. The unexpected – since

34

when could you trust it? As he presses his forehead against the glass the senior lecturer goes over it again. The best teacher a boy could have? Yes, this life is certainly coming apart at the seams. Birds are falling out of the sky in north London. As a negative indicator, that can hardly be topped. Except, of course, by the blood.

PART THREE

Semaphore

THEY ARE IN A PUB AT AROUND DUSK. Correction – they are in the large annex of a public house in West Hampstead just as the lights are coming on. This annex, which looks much like a church hall, is given over tonight, as it is every Thursday, to a popular line dancing session that is free to join. There must be fifty or sixty people – men and women of all ages and all shapes and sizes – arranged in a kind of regimental grid formation and spaced a few feet apart from wall to wall within the annex, which connects to the pub itself via a short corridor housing the toilets. All the men in this room wear plaid or checked or tartan shirts – all, that is, except one.

'I'm really not sure about this,' Donaldson comments, glancing backwards over his shoulder. 'I don't think I'm quite ready for this particular cultural delight.'

'You'll be fine,' Nathan tells him from a few feet behind. 'Why don't you change places with me so you can at least watch what I'm doing? Relax and enjoy. Just remember – step, rock back, recover, right shift, cross, unwind, left shift, rock back, recover. Then simply repeat from the top.'

'To repeat any programme,' Donaldson says, 'suggests having successfully completed it in the first instance. Let *me* repeat – I think this is a dangerous recreational mistake.'

'Try to forget who you are for five goddamn minutes, professor. That's all it takes.'

'Five minutes is quite a long time. Try counting it out.'

'You like country music, don't you? So, just go with it.'

'Let me see, now. Islands In The Stream, anyone? Kenny and Dolly over and over again?'

'Islands In The Stream may well feature at some point. It often does. Based on the posthumous novel by Hemingway, right?'

'Just the title, one imagines, smart arse. Oh, lord – give me the strength to do thy work.'

It turns out the senior lecturer has seriously misjudged his most promising student in multiple ways. When the dancing is over, they repair to the pub in order to drink more beer. It turns out Nathan doesn't have any parents, enlightened or otherwise, with whom to make those annual road trips to Rincón or Puerto Escondido when the surf is up. The sponsored student, whose school fees are met by an obscure American foundation, has no blood brothers or sisters, unless it is in a once removed kind of way. He is an orphan who has been raised by his uncle and aunt in a respectable commuter town to the south of the capital and, for a few formative years, in Seattle, Washington.

'They never really loved me,' he tells Donaldson. 'I mean they had their own kids to love. But I'm not complaining. I get a cheque from them at Christmas. Sixty quid, in case you're wondering.'

'I'm not,' Donaldson says. 'Do you think about your parents at all these days?'

'No,' Nathan says. 'I never knew them so I have nothing to go on in terms of memories.'

'In that case you don't have to worry about how much to love or be loved. That's a major plus, believe me.'

'Do you have children, Don? I'm guessing you do. A boy and a girl —'

Time passes quickly. As the hours come and go, Donaldson is forced to accept that Nathan Ford won't be sloping off to a hotel in Tottenham Court Road any time soon. What does it mean for the father and husband? It means his wife of fifteen years is spending tonight with her artist cousin in order to help him make a will. And Donaldson doesn't quite know how he feels about that. Strange – he almost feels let down by the way things are. He had taken it for granted that his life was lurching, or *lurching further*, off the rails, but now it seems he has one less thing to worry about. Nathan gets up – he is going to the toilet and then to the bar. The jukebox is playing a honkytonk song. When Donaldson checks his phone, he discovers a message from Tamara. She is at Jamie's place in Kilburn. That is not a surprise to Donaldson – not any more. But what comes next is surprising. Tamara is going to be at Jamie's place for more than one night. She is going to be there, she indicates, for a little while. She has moved out of the house, taking Alice with her. Oh, and she plans to call Donaldson tomorrow to discuss this whole situation.

When Nathan returns with two beers, Donaldson already has his jacket on. Now he zips it up.

'Did I say something wrong?' Nathan asks, setting down the streaming bottles.

'Not at all,' Donaldson says. 'I'm sorry – I have to go. I've just had a message from my wife telling me she's leaving me tonight, as in *leaving* me. I think I need to make a few calls.'

'That's too bad. I mean – I'm sorry to hear that.'

'Oh, I think it's been on the cards for quite some time. I'm just thinking about the kids, that's all.'

'She isn't taking them with her?'

38

'Looks like she's taking one of them – the younger one.'

'Leaving you to look after the older one?'

'Something along those lines.'

'Like I say – that's too bad. I was about to invite you to come home with me tonight, but I guess that's not going to happen now.'

'I beg your pardon. Are you propositioning me, Nathan Ford?'

'Well, yes – I believe that's the technical term.'

And then Donaldson feels doubly bad about life. He is running out on something here. He can't help that. It is clear in his head – he is not running *away* from something, or anything. But he has to leave. 'Look –' he says. 'It's been great. It's been a blast, but I have to go now. I'll see you in school. I'm not going to give you a speech about professional conduct, or misconduct, or any of that. Let's just say you're not my type. In any case, I'm probably old enough to be your father – if you had one.'

'Maybe that's the whole idea,' Nathan says, shrugging lightly.

'I'm sorry,' Donaldson says. 'That came out all wrong. Do you forgive me?'

'Of course. You'd better run along. Oh, and Don – there's no need to worry.'

'About what?'

'Dexter Doolittle. I'll be sure to give him a happy ending –'

Outside in the street he takes a deep breath. In fact, he takes a few deep breaths. It is raining heavily after a prolonged dry spell – now the smell of damp dust is in the air. How Donaldson wishes he had gone to the toilet before leaving the pub. But there is no going back from here. He must go forward, whatever that takes, whatever it means. He takes out his phone and brings up his wife's number. Then he changes his mind about calling Tamara. What exactly does he have to say to her? It occurs to him she is just a modest distance away in Kilburn. Odd that they should be so close to each other at this hour. They are almost close enough for semaphore, Donaldson reasons. It is chucking it down now. People run for cover, freesheets and magazines held over their heads. Donaldson brings up Henry's mobile phone number in place of his wife's, but when he calls his son, it goes straight to voicemail. Just as the father is about to blurt out something foolish and heartfelt – *I love you*, for example – a white van flashes past at speed and throws a shower of muddy rainwater at him. He is without an umbrella in this part of north London.

ON SATURDAY DONALDSON CALLS round to the flat in Kilburn. It takes him an hour and a half using three different trains both above and below ground to reach his destination on this sultry morning, first day of the new month. It is his intention to take Alice swimming as usual – his daughter is on the cusp of mastering the poolside dive *sans splash*. But nothing is usual at this time.

Tamara's cousin, a struggling artist plucked from the books of central casting, inhabits a downbeat apartment above commercial premises on Shoot Up Hill, part of the major thoroughfare running roughly north from Marble Arch towards Scotland. Donaldson has been here before – just the once, on the occasion of Jamie's thirtieth, when the uneasy peace that existed, that still exists, between writer and artist was put to the test, or laid on the line, or stretched to the limit. It is possible they share a fear of death or chronic disease. But the truth is Jamie resents Donaldson in a disappointing way that has to do with money or social status or looks – in other words, the most important things. At least, that is how Donaldson perceives it, and he is probably right. For his part, the writer hates the very idea that he might regard himself for just one second as more successful, or smarter, or better in any conceivable way, than the creator of these nightmarish visions in mixed media rejected by every gallery in the capital over twenty years and more. Now he presses the buzzer at street level. When a response comes, he can't hear it – there is a big red omnibus waiting at the lights within spitting distance of Jamie's distressed front door. Suddenly the door gives, and Donaldson is in a long, dark passage which leads to an internal door and the stairs, and which smells strongly even at this hour of curry.

'How's Henry?' she asks straight off in the galley kitchen at the front of the flat where the noise from the traffic below is an egregious constant. 'Is he coping all right with just you around?'

'He's OK, I think. I mean – it's not as if he could move in here anyway. How many rooms are there – aside from the tiny one that's piled floor to ceiling with screaming canvases?'

'He could share with Jamie. I'm sure it's only for a short time.'

'There are two things there. First, Henry won't be sharing with Jamie. Second, have you made a plan that I should know about?'

At this time Tamara busies herself with opening the cupboards and taking certain items out and putting others back with the result that she doesn't see Alice loom palely from the darkness at the heart of the flat. It is so very stuffy in here today, the mother is probably thinking, yet she fails to open a window on account of the appalling racket and pollution rising up from the street.

'Hello, princess,' the father says, patting a bag at his shoulder. 'All set to go swimming with Daddy?' She stands in a gloomy space outside the bedrooms and the windowless bathroom. The daughter is on the landing, the parents are in the narrow kitchen, one behind the other. Donaldson turns towards his wife. 'Don't worry,' he says. 'I left the Renault at home. We'll take a train. God knows there are enough stations to choose from.' Then he turns to Alice. 'Shall we catch a choo-choo train today, princess?'

41

'I'm not a princess, silly,' Alice drawls. 'And I don't want to go swimming with you any more.'

'Have you been briefing against me, wife of fifteen years?' asks Donaldson, once Alice has taken herself back to the room she now shares with her mother.

'It's her birthday next Saturday,' Tamara says, 'in case you've forgotten.'

'I haven't forgotten,' Donaldson insists. 'Henry's is coming up soon, too, if I'm not mistaken. So, do we know what Alice wants – from dearest Mummy and Daddy?'

'She wants a budgie,' Tamara says, ignoring his provocation.

'A budgie? As in a caged bird? I don't think we can let her have a fucking *budgie*. Do you?'

'I think we should give her whatever she says she wants, under the circumstances.'

'The circumstances? I think you'll find the circumstances are not of my making.'

'No? Think about that for just a moment. Don't you see it? We haven't made love for six months, Don. We haven't had sex for six months. Seasons have come and gone. Rivers have run dry –'

'Is that what this is about?' he asks defensively. There – she has said it finally. He has waited such a long time for this hour to arrive, and now he discovers he has nothing to say for himself. He has no excuse to offer his wife. He no longer wants to be intimate with her. Is it a sin, or a crime? She accepts no blame, it seems, but that is of little consequence to Donaldson. He is a man – the fault is his. And she is very busy. She is busy saving lives and such like. Has she been counting the months? Perhaps she has been quietly crossing off the months so as to hold the shocking tally against him when the time feels right. There is the blood, of course, but he won't mention that.

The blood is not an excuse – it is a private matter between him and his urologist. It is proof of something on him – a spot or a stain. The blood is a metaphor – Donaldson sees this without really looking. It is more than mere *blood*. It is a sign of something deficient in him – an inadequacy of feeling, say, or an insufficiency of love.

'You should probably go now,' Tamara says. 'Don't you have exercise books to mark? Kindly tell Henry I'll expect him here on Tuesday straight after school. And tell him Alice wants him to teach her the *bloody* Selkirk grace.'

There is a pet shop in Muswell Hill that sells budgerigars in a variety of vivid colours from stock. These birds should be lively and sociable and, ideally, not too young when purchased. Donaldson discovers all this and much more from his phone. There are certain accessories and accoutrements to be bought, of course, along with the birds themselves. These items have to do with keeping the little darlings happy and healthy for the duration of their confinement. Small mirrors, swings and cuttlefish bones head up Donaldson's list of must-haves here. Before all else there is the question of the setting, or the environment, or the domain. The cage is key. In the matter of keeping a bird confined to quarters over long periods of time, the cage has a life and death role to play.

After he regains street level at Camden Town station, he heads northwards through the sprawling clothes stalls until he reaches the covered bazaar on the Chalk Farm side of the famous market. It is here in a cavernous import-export emporium that he finds what he is looking for suspended from the ceiling along with others just like it in small, medium and large sizes. The dome-shaped cage, which is made beautifully from a type of thick gold wire, is big. You might describe it as spacious if you were a young metropolitan budgerigar rooming alone. The wires of the frame are spaced nicely apart. Too close together and the immature bird might sicken. Too wide apart and the chances increase of a bid for freedom.

'How much is the large bird cage?' Donaldson calls out. 'I can't read the price tag from down here.'

'The large one is sixty pounds,' says a disembodied voice from behind a ziggurat of Moroccan pouffes.

Sixty quid is daylight robbery. Sixty quid is what Nathan Ford gets from his adoptive parents at Christmas, Donaldson tells himself with a stab of something like respect for the student who surprised him and then surprised him again. When he harks back to the time they spent together in a West Hampstead public house, or its dance hall annex, his recollection has the texture and logic of a morning dream, and this excites him unaccountably in the present moment. He is chuffed with his bird cage choice. This is an exceptional cage by any reasonable measure. In terms of its generous proportions, in particular, it is satisfactory, Donaldson decides, digging a card from his wallet. He has a horror, recently acquired, of dead birds.

ON THE MORNING OF ALICE'S BIRTHDAY, Donaldson takes her to the municipal pool at Swiss Cottage. If she has changed her mind about declining these Saturday morning swimming invitations it is almost certainly on account of her birthday present, a cute, yellow budgerigar in a delightful gilded cage.

'Will you help me pick a name for it, Daddy?' she asks sweetly as they peer down at the still diving pool – open today for reasons unknown – through the glass wall of the reception area high above the water. The daughter has already posed this question about the bird's name in the stuffy kitchen of the flat in Kilburn. She repeats it now because she hasn't yet had a convincing answer. 'What is it, anyway – a boy budgie or a girl budgie?'

'You mean a cock or a hen. When we talk about budgerigars we talk about a cock or a hen.'

Yes, he is an expert these days. He will leave the naming to his wife. He is an expert on seed, and the master of feed in general. He has an opinion on bathing and beak scrubbing and budgie hygiene quite widely. Outside the changing area he has the usual dilemma. Should Alice change alone in the women's room or with him in the men's zone? They should really have a third space, a neutral space, Donaldson concludes, making a mental note to raise the issue with persons unspecified at an hour unscheduled, and knowing he will never do that particular thing. It is all right. Everything is OK. His dilemma is resolved unexpectedly when Alice informs him that she is perfectly capable of changing by herself now that she is *ten*. And, in point of fact, her tone suggests, he should really have worked that out for himself. It is true she has developed a tendency to wrongfoot him. One day she seems younger than her age, the next older. This might very easily be an *older* day, Donaldson decides optimistically. That a new swimming pool era has begun is confirmed – Alice has brought her own pound coin for the lockers.

In the changing room he meets nice Mr Sobers, a pool regular who is on a personal mission to get black children, and not least his own brood, to swim.

'They don't want to get their cornrows wet,' he tells Donaldson with a high-pitched giggle. 'They don't seem to understand it might save their life one day – or someone else's life, for that matter.'

'Don't they teach them in school these days?' asks Donaldson mildly, pinning his locker key to his shorts.

'They haven't taught mine – not yet. I'm thinking maybe they can opt out in certain circumstances, you know. Anyway – the wife is here with me today. This is a war, Mr Donaldson, a war.'

When he arrives at the pool there is no sign of Alice. No doubt she will need a little longer to change today. Since Donaldson has a few minutes in hand, a few moments to spare, he does what he has wanted to do for a while. He walks calmly and purposefully towards the diving platforms located on the far side of the diving pool. When he gets there, he doesn't hesitate. He climbs the steps to the middle board, the three-metre springboard. Above him is the upper deck, the top tier. Now Donaldson climbs the ladder that leads to the high pasture. From here he can actually see through the glass wall to the reception area with its Coca-Cola machine and snack machine. He checks – there is no one in the water below. As he composes himself overlooking the pool, he hears his daughter call out to him from far off. Soon he launches up and out at the same time, then lowers his head and stretches his arms in front of him. The weight of his head dropping down between his arms brings his body – his torso, then his legs – into vertical alignment just before he enters the water. His feet are together, his toes pointed – this is the last box he ticks before he closes his eyes and goes under, meaning *through*, what is there.

They are at the side of the main pool, at the deep end. Things are not going so well today in respect of Alice's diving lessons. She is travelling backwards it seems to Donaldson. She is heading in the wrong direction. Her feet are slightly apart when she cuts through the surface of the water. True – there is very little splash on display. But the feet must be together, with the toes pointed. That is the way it has always been since diving was invented. Now she has begun to cry – a silent, sullen type of crying that is hard to countenance and harder still to counter.

'I'm not sure you're really trying today, Alice,' says Donaldson, looking down at his daughter and rubbing his upper arms. 'Are you doing this on purpose to make Daddy cross?'

46

As he watches Alice's pained face dip down below the water, Donaldson feels a hand on his shoulder. It is nice Mr Sobers who wants the unlicensed diving teacher to come and meet his wife. She is in the big pool at the shallow end with one of their children, a girl slightly older than Alice.

'Dido won't put her head under,' the mother explains, rocking back and forth in the water while sweeping her hands respectfully across its surface. 'Do you have any tips for her, Mr Donaldson, I wonder? My husband says you're quite the swimmer.'

'And *diver*,' puts in Sobers admiringly. 'I saw you just now.'

He is in a swimming pool filled with salt water – with sea water, that is. There comes the cry of a gull, or similar. This is somewhere in the south of France. His father forces his head below the surface of the water. The father's hand presses down on his son's neck. The boy is crying, but his tears are worth less than zero down here. He can hear his father's voice in the pristine air just above. The father counts out the seconds from one to ten. Will it be enough to satisfy? Will ten seconds be sufficient under the circumstances? A sea horse is present in a salt water pool – that is what the son will recall when he starts to dream about this incident at another time of life and in a different place altogether.

'Tips?' he says doubtfully, addressing the girl directly. 'I don't know about tips exactly. There are three things to think about – the face, the head and the eyes. Try putting your face in the water with your eyes shut. Do that a few times. It's not so difficult. Then drop down so that your whole head is under the water. Do it here at the shallow end. You can hold your nose closed if you want to. The last thing is to open your eyes underwater. It doesn't hurt at all. It feels quite natural. Try counting out the seconds inside your head while you look around you. When you get as far as ten – well, then you've

47

done it.' He is about to turn away, his work over, when the mother shrieks and points towards the diving boards. Now Donaldson hears a voice he recognises, a voice he knows, come from far away.

'Daddy!'

She is at the front edge of the topmost station. She looks small and pale up there. She has made up her mind about this, it would seem. Now she launches herself headfirst from the platform without more ado. That's right – she doesn't jump, she dives. Her technique being poor, she fails to push upwards with head raised for the first part of her dive, with the result that her head comes down too soon and her legs go over the top, over the vertical axis, the key meridian. What happens is that she executes a more or less perfect somersault. As she enters the water with a little cry, her feet are together.

He has been unable to move. Now he runs towards the nearest corner of the pool. As he rounds the corner he slips on the wet tiles. He gets up right away. His leg is cut, or badly grazed. It should hurt like hell, but he barely notices it. When he reaches the diving pool, he stops at the edge of the water. Alice is at the surface, waving.

'Did I make a splash?' she calls out to him.

He falls into the water. He falls in and drops to the bottom at the deepest part of the diving pool. There is blood in the water now. There is not much blood – just enough to interest a pelagic shark at a distance of, say, one nautical mile. Is he dying? Has he been dying for a while? It strikes Donaldson he might be dying without feeling it, which is a cheap way to go about the whole transformative thing. At roughly twenty feet under, all air exhaled, he squats on the white tiles and counts to ten as slowly as he can.

Now a most eloquent silence sits within him. This silence – an outrider for eternal rest, perhaps, or the aftermath of the senseless tolling of the bell of world peace – is inside his head and heart both.

It looks as if Mrs Sobers has wrapped Alice up in a great big fluffy pink towel. Donaldson lies flat on his back on the tiles at the edge of the diving pool with a capable first-aider kneeling beside him and a worried lifeguard hovering above. When he shuts his eyes he sees the lonely sea horse – his friend and confessor. Soon he hears young Dido Sobers call out excitedly. 'I did it, Mum. I made it to ten –'

NO NEW ENTRIES IN DAD'S DIARY. I don't know what that means. Is it a good sign or a bad sign? Perhaps he has simply been too busy separating from his wife to keep up his blood diary. Maybe he can't bear to talk about it any more, even to himself. Could it be his irony well has run dry? He has had a letter from the hospital – I saw it on the doormat along with an electricity bill and a members' magazine from the Tate. As a piece of circumstantial evidence, the letter must remain inconclusive. I can root around inside Dad's computer until the cows come home, but I cannot open his mail.

For the record – I don't miss my mother from day to day, and I don't miss my sister either. At least, not much. At first, I felt guilty about this, but then I flipped the coin. I began to wonder how much they'll miss me. Mum did take me aside in order to ask me if I was hurting within. I told her I didn't really understand what she meant by that. If I am hurting inside it is probably because my lucky clinic in Belsize Park is to close its doors after being judged unhelpful, or helpful in the wrong way. The short-term effect of this development is to refocus my campaign while bolstering my resolve.

We turn our attention here necessarily to the Sandie Shaw Fan Club (SSFC), of which I am a founder member, and whose presence has already been noted in this document. The club exists to honour the achievements in song of a talent of yesteryear. In fact, for us the musical flame burns just as brightly today. In order to retain access

49

to this exclusive coterie, members must submit to an ongoing series of initiation tests, many of them physical in nature. (There is a whiff of ritual humiliation in all this – that goes without saying.) One such examination involves being hung upside down in a toilet while the flush is activated harshly. Elsewhere, the neophyte is asked to recite the lyrics of two out of three songs – Long Live Love, Tomorrow, and Girl Don't Come. The evergreen Puppet On A String, deemed by consensus too *slight*, is ineligible. These efforts matter. The least error of phrasing here means falling at the first hurdle.

The fact that the Sandie Shaw Fan Club is a mostly harmless front for a very different type of society has the power to shock me still. Advanced members are committed to, and preparing for, the taking of their own life by one of several practical means allocated by peer review. Thus, we have Jarvis (carbon monoxide poisoning in garage), Ogilvie (fatal descent from tall structure), and Marshall (person under a train at Kentish Town station) in the current van of our operations. Add to that list one Henry Donaldson (suicide by suspension), and the stage is set for the foreseeable future. There is a twist here that is worth mentioning. According to the rules of the Sandie Shaw Fan Club, persons looking to swap this life for another must do so before their sixteenth birthday. Time is running out for me. I will be the first to go. In many ways it is a privilege to be first. Should others choose to step away from their responsibilities after my departure, there will be little I can do about it.

Note on method. I will need two belts. One is not enough. The first belt is fastened to the second in order to provide the structural means. I have my own belt, of course. And I have sourced a second belt from a neglected corner of Dad's wardrobe, this fine example being attached to a pair of purple corduroy trousers he has long ago banished to the Outer Mongolia of memory.

We have been eating a lot of takeaways – Chinese, Indian and Turkish, on a rotating basis. If Dad is dying you wouldn't know it. He fairly wolfs it all down. Or does that signify he is hollowing out inside? He hasn't asked any more questions relating to the famous cricket pavilion bullying episode. Soon, of course, his son's mental health status will move centre stage in a startling new way. There will be no note. There can be no note – that is in the rule book of the Sandie Shaw Fan Club. No matter – this diary will do the job very well. And Dad will discover my diary, just as I have found his. I trust him to figure it out. I rely on him to intuit that my computer password is exactly the same as his.

ON WEDNESDAY MORNING, half an hour before his writing class is scheduled to begin, Donaldson is summoned by text message to the principal's office in the administration block at Queen Anne's. This comes towards the end of the second semester and towards the start of the summer holiday. The senior lecturer is certainly tired. He is weary of teaching and living, and his left leg – damaged in a recent poolside accident – hurts like hell.

'I can see you're limping,' says the principal, a short, interested woman who combines the roles of MBE, cigar smoker, Italophile and Katherine Mansfield scholar with her regular curricular duties centred on this cool, dark office, and whom Donaldson happens to like very much. 'What transpired?'

'I kicked a football for the first time in ten years and managed to bugger my knee.' He has no idea why he feels a need to lie to the principal about his leg. Clearly, it is a kind of defence mechanism – that is the *what* of it. But why? Is this even a lie? Lie is too strong a word, Donaldson decides, accepting the offer of a seat on this side of the desk where a wall of ledgers and lever arch files threatens to topple. Then it hits him. He did the same thing at a birthday party once upon a time when he claimed his wife of a decade and a half had chosen a certain paperback novel as a gift. This is not lying, he concludes now. This is not even fibbing. This is dissembling. It is a necessary dissimulation in the face of a hostile world. A man should hold back something of himself – how else to pay the toll at midnight on the bridge of desire and regret? 'I never did like ball games.'

'But my dear fellow –' the principal says. 'Don't you know all sport is ruinous to the imagination?'

'The way masturbating used to be?' Donaldson says, enjoying the ironic juxtaposition on one side of the office of gurgling fish tank with statement exercise bike. 'Ah, those were the days.'

'Are you all right, Don?'

'Of course.' Now it begins, or proceeds – the world come to pay him a visit. 'Don't I look all right?'

'It's my unhappy duty to report,' the principal says, taking up spectacles and eyeing an A4 print-out, 'that someone has made an anonymous accusation of sexual misconduct against you.'

'An anonymous accusation?'

'That's right. Via a post on the school's intranet.'

'When an accusation is unattributed, or unattributable, how is one to take it seriously?' He thinks fast and hard – of course he does. Of the charge he is innocent – he knows that well enough. But who is it that seeks to undo him?

'I agree with you there,' the principal says, wagging spectacles characteristically. 'Would you like the good news now? In the self-same thread a certain Donald Donaldson is further mentioned in despatches – this time as the best teacher a boy could have.'

'Oh, that's generous of someone.' There is Nathan and there is Melanie, both students spurned by their esteemed teacher on this or that recent occasion. Either of these two could have posted the bad news, but in point of fact only one of them can be responsible for the good. 'That's a nice thing to say, isn't it?'

'Be careful, please, Don. Don't get caught out on a misconduct rap by a disaffected student. You know I wouldn't be able to protect you if it came right down to her word against yours.'

'Or his word, for that matter.'

'As you say – or *his* word. Have you ever entertained the notion that one day this office might be yours?'

'Frankly, no. The neon tetras I can live with quite happily, but the exercise bike really has to go.'

In class he is saddened by the general scene. Melanie is present, studiously averting her gaze in a way that has guilty written all over it. The desk usually taken by Nathan Ford is unoccupied.

'Does anyone know where he is?' Donaldson asks. He already sees it for what it is. His most promising student has withdrawn from the class for reasons of identity, or integrity, or out of resentment or something else. 'Is he OK, does anyone know?'

And here there is a kind of communal shrugging of shoulders within the classroom, as if to suggest that no one really cares about Nathan Ford any more. If he is not here, he is nowhere.

'Sorry, Don,' says Melanie, eyeing a part of the world located slightly to one side of his head. 'I heard he transferred to the Angela Carter course for the last few weeks of term.'

'That Angela Carter programme,' Siobhan adds knowingly, 'is *terribly* popular with the ladies.'

'And so it should be,' Donaldson points out. He is very tired. Can he keep this up for just a few more sessions? 'Dylan – you were pencilled to read the latest from your film scenario today, were you not? Your impossibly talented recording artist is in the throes of a

53

bitter divorce, which just happens to coincide with his most creative period to date. Am I right?' He doesn't listen to young Dylan. He cannot actually hear young Dylan. A songbird is doing its beautiful best to distract him – this from the foliage beyond the sash window. What species of bird is it that can drown out the noise of the world with the simplest refrain? It is all Donaldson can do to stop himself marching directly to the window and flinging it open. Abruptly, he finds himself presiding over an unscripted silence in the classroom. 'Excellent, excellent –' he adjudges quickly from behind the lectern. 'And now we turn our attention to Joseph Conrad for the last time in our happy programme. Was he a racist, as Achebe has famously argued? That is the motion for tomorrow's fifteen-minute debate. Siobhan has agreed to speak against the motion – we thank you for that, Siobhan. But who will speak *for*? Sort it out between you by tomorrow, please. I don't want to have to do the job again myself – I don't get paid enough. OK – that's a wrap, campers.'

After the classroom has emptied, Donaldson stands at the open sash window, looking for a songbird. There is no point in taking the matter up with Melanie. The whole Melanie episode is just one of those things as far as Donaldson is concerned. It is the world come to pay him a visit. He looks for the songbird in the tree. Funny – he has never been remotely interested in birdsong until now. He listens hard for the bird, but the bird has flown. The yellow flowers of the manicured bushes beside the bicycle racks below are in full display. Suddenly, Donaldson thinks of Alice's budgie – the colours do it for him. Has it been christened yet, his daughter's pet? Does it have a name? Is it happy? It is just a sense he has. Donaldson can't be sure, of course – even the truth is provisional now. It is just a bad feeling he carries with him from hour to hour and which won't quit.

PART FOUR

Forces Unknown

NOW IT IS TOMORROW. WHEN Donaldson rises, he can tell Henry is still at home. In other words, Henry has not yet left for school, which is most unusual – the youth is fastidious in all areas, including affairs of the clock. When Donaldson knocks at the bedroom door, he discovers his son is feeling unwell today. No, there is no need to call the school. The boy may yet rally and go forth.

He is on Blackstock Road, limping due north towards Finsbury Park station. He has a bad feeling in his heart. This feeling is always there now, but today it is even more *there* than usual. Is it Henry? It must be Henry, who is never ill. The boy never gets sick, but today he is poorly. Donaldson tries to remember the last time his son was unwell – he can't recall a time. Now he considers turning back. He is minded to return to the house in order to take care of his beloved son, but he forces himself to go on. This is when he is roughly level with the old Arsenal stadium – the commercial area lies ahead. To turn back now would be silly – his son would be the first to say that. It is at the junction with Seven Sisters Road that he sees it – a white van peeling off towards Highbury, towards the house. There comes a flash of light from the windscreen of the van. Naturally, there is a flash of light – it means Donaldson is unable to see the driver's face as the van accelerates past him heading south.

He is decided. As he hops and skips down Blackstock Road he drags his hurt leg behind him. He tosses his bag, heavy with books, over a low wall in front of a house with a red door. Red door spells danger. What sort of danger, though? Donaldson doesn't know. He only knows he has to get home before white van man smashes the windscreen of the faithful Renault, or slashes its tyres, or sets fire to the whole vehicle right outside the house. Now his leg is killing him, and there is a pain in his chest. The good people stare at him. They step sideways on the pavement in order to let him pass. Six minutes later Donaldson is back outside his house. The Renault – it is right there. It is exactly where it should be. This car looks OK. This car looks to be intact. What is more – there is no white van to be seen anywhere. There is something else, however – an odd movement in the hall of the house glimpsed through the frosted glass panel of the front door. It must be Henry, of course, who is responsible for that unusual movement high up in the hallway.

At the exact moment Donaldson opens the front door, Henry kicks away the step ladder he has been standing on in order to hang himself from the banister at the very top of the stairs. What occurs now is that a dual spindle arrangement crashes to earth along with Henry and two leather belts that are attached to his neck or throat. Unfortunately, the young man bangs his head on the edge of a step during his awkward descent with the result that he is unconscious and bleeding when Donaldson lifts him up and carries him through to the table in the second reception room. After he has removed the belts from around his son's neck, Donaldson checks to make sure the boy is still breathing, which he is. The father takes a clean dish towel from the kitchen drawer and wraps it around Henry's head. Then he finds his phone and calls an ambulance. Next, he calls his wife of fifteen years and leaves a brief, calm message asking her to call him back as soon as she can. Finally, he returns the step ladder to a cupboard under the stairs and clears up the mess in the hall.

In the brief time it takes for an ambulance to arrive, Donaldson busies himself looking for the note. The fact that there is no note to be found either upstairs or downstairs pains the father grievously – he is actually being sick at the kitchen sink when they ring the bell. It could be that the note is hidden about Henry's person, of course, but Donaldson is unwilling to ransack the body in order to find it.

At the hospital he waits for two hours before being told his son is conscious and not in any immediate danger. When they ask him what happened, he tells them Henry fell down the stairs, which is a version of the truth. When they ask about the bruises on the youth's neck, Donaldson shrugs and offers nothing. Here, he thinks only of the boy's state of mind. All the while he wants to ask them the only thing worth asking. Did you find it? Did you find the note? When he asks if he can see his son, they inform him Henry has specifically asked to see his mother at this time. And here is Tamara, right on cue. She rushes down this institutional corridor – soon she will burst through the courtroom doors and create a minor sensation for the benefit of the reporters in the gallery.

'Oh, Don,' she says, still breathing hard, when they are alone together. 'Is he OK? Is he all right?'

'He's all right,' Donaldson manages to tell her. He is about to say *he's going to be fine*, or words to that effect, as they invariably do in tear-jerker films, but it strikes him that there is no way of knowing as much for certain at this stage in the proceedings. When he thinks of all the difficult questions he must shortly put to his son he doesn't know where to begin. In his heart he knows these questions should be obvious, if not exactly easy, under the circumstances. 'He wants to see you first. He specifically asked to see you rather than me.'

'Really?' Tamara says doubtfully. 'Was it something at school? You didn't tell me what happened.'

'That's because I didn't know how to tell you,' Donaldson says. Something is knocking at the door of his consciousness – or is it his conscience? It's a surprising thing, a miraculous thing, even, when seen in a certain light. It has to do with Henry and what befell him today. Now it comes to Donaldson in an oddly chilling way – thanks to a late intervention on the part of forces unknown he himself was present at the very instant his son failed to take his own life. How fateful is that? Yes, the banister played a meaningful role. Respect the woodwork. What if it hadn't collapsed when it did? In fact, these forces are not *quite* unknown to Donald Donaldson, are they? White van man has struck again. What exactly does he *want* with all this? 'Shall I tell you the whole story now?' the husband asks his wife.

THE IDEA THAT HIS SON would make a determined attempt on his own life on the eve of his sixteenth birthday haunts the father. He understands it will always be that way. Nothing can make up for an event such as this one. Nothing can undo what has been done – not now, not ever. Standing at the black door of the flat in Kilburn, his shorts and goggles rolled up in a towel under his arm, Donaldson considers for the first time in his life the possibility that his son might predecease him. In the corridor beyond the front door the air stings his eyes using rare spices from the orient. A utility bill in his wife's name lies on the bubbling linoleum half way down the hall. What does it mean? Donaldson picks up the bill and takes it upstairs with him. It means she has no plans to come home any time soon.

The budgerigar is dead. Alice's budgie – known as Joey for the most recent chapter of its short history – lies on a mattress of cotton wool in a Puma shoe box on the worktop beside the hob. Not only is Alice unwilling to go swimming with her father this day – she also refuses to speak to him. In fact, she hasn't uttered a word since she discovered Joey on the floor of the lovely cage at around dawn, the bird lying inert on its back with claws raised pathetically in the air.

'She screamed,' Tamara tells Donaldson in the stuffy kitchen. 'Since then, not a peep out of her.'

'We'll just have to bury it,' Donaldson tells his wife. 'Why don't you tell Alice I'll bury it in the garden at home?'

'Will you stay for lunch?' Tamara asks him.

'Is your cousin here today?' he asks her.

'No,' she says. 'Jamie has some kind of girlfriend or lover these days.'

'All right, then,' he says.

They eat standing up in the kitchen. She has made a spaghetti ragù with a few peas in it – the way they do it in Sicily, Donaldson reminds her needlessly while in his mind's eye he roves a charming trattoria, shady and with gingham tablecloths, they twice lunched at in Palermo when they were younger and happier in life.

'Will you go to the hospital today?' she says at last.

'Between four and six,' he says. 'And on Monday morning if they'll let me.'

'I'll go tomorrow, then,' she says.

'Will you come home when he gets out?' he asks. 'I don't think this is good for Alice either, by the way.'

'You might as well know –' she says. 'I'm seeing someone else.'

'Oh,' he says. 'How long has that been going on?'

'Not long,' she says. 'Look – we have to talk about Henry now. What you don't know is that he wants to transition.' Here, she runs cold water from the kitchen tap into two red beakers from an Esso promotion. 'Do you understand what I'm saying?'

59

'Henry wants to transition to a girl? To a woman?'

'He doesn't feel able to talk to you about it. Imagine that –'

'I can imagine that. I can understand that.'

'You're a selfish man, Don. Do you know that? You're a selfish, complacent, arrogant, vain man. Now your son doesn't even want to talk to you. I'm not sure he ever did. You need to find your son before it's too late. And get someone in to fix the banister, for God's sake. I mean before he gets back –'

He has never regarded himself as selfish or complacent or vain. Is that what she means – the fact that he has never actually thought about it? 'It sounds like my son wants to be something else now,' he says. He is not much hurt by his wife's character summary. Neither does he reel from this latest news about Henry. He has sunk so low in the past thirty-six hours there is little that is capable of shocking him. 'Son, daughter – same difference, if you ask me.' And now he makes no sense – not even to himself. Especially not to himself. Just the day before yesterday he failed to recognise his child as a suicide risk. How could such a father hope or expect to understand *anything at all* about his only begotten son? Then it comes out. It pops out. 'He didn't leave a note, Tamara. He wasn't even going to leave us a note. Can you imagine such a wretched and lonely state of affairs? It's just a heart-breaking thing –'

In the middle part of the afternoon he takes a trowel from the shed and digs as deep a hole as he can at the bottom of the garden beside a concrete buddha green with moss. He places the dead bird roughly ten inches down with its back to the centre of the earth and its beak pointing up at the sky. He has never been one for prayers or praying – now Donaldson rattles off the Selkirk grace in his head. This absurdity he indulges for his daughter's sake only – if she is prepared to dive off the high platform for him, then he is more than happy to do her this service in return. After he fills in the hole with the clay-claggy soil, a robin comes to peck over the site of the grave, which is dark with disturbed earth.

At around four he sets out on foot for the Whittington Hospital in Archway with a bunch of freesias, three bars of Toblerone, and a paperback collection of Guardian cryptic crossword puzzles in a plastic Sainsbury's bag. Also in the bag are Henry's laptop, charger and headphones. It has occurred to the father he might try to access his son's computer in a search for mental health clues. Would that be right? Would it even be possible? In the hospital shop he buys a black ballpoint pen. Some gifts, he decides, must be gender neutral from now on. Waiting for the lift he gets to thinking again. His wife of fifteen years is seeing someone else, as in a film. How much does he care about that on a scale of one to ten? Seven? Five? Three? In the lift he gives the flowers to a girl about Alice's age.

DAD CAME TO SEE ME TODAY. He brought my computer and some presents and stayed for as long as he could bear to. He looked sad, as befits the guardian of a suicide risk. I am the child who tried and failed to take his own life. I will forever be that boy – unless I am that *girl*. Dad didn't mention it at all, the elephant in the room, even though I asked Mum to tell him of my intentions. No doubt he is waiting for me to bring the subject up in my own time and my own way. Could it be he has managed to access my computer? If so, he already knows everything there is to know. Actually, that is one of his pet sayings – *a man must know everything*. But the truth is he can never know everything. Why would a boy intent on transitioning to a girl try to take his own life in the meantime? That is the question Dad can never really answer. No one can answer it – no one else. To me it's simple. It even has a perverse logic. There is the ultimate self-harm and then there is the transitioning. These two things are related to each other in a causal way. In other words, if I pulled off the first, I wouldn't have to deal with the second. This relationship holds reassuringly today – it remains the case that the one obviates the possibility of, or need for, the other.

Thematically speaking, this business of my transitioning might be regarded as the *second* elephant in the room – that is if you count my failed attempt to kill myself with two belts, one step ladder, and a newel post. (I know the technical term for the wooden bollard at the top of the stairs only because I googled it as part of my botched preparations.) I know some will argue forcefully that it is impossible not to hang yourself unequivocally from a decent newel post, which is designed expressly not to collapse. Others will suggest slyly that I must have deliberately attached my second belt to the fey spindles instead of the doughty handrail. Still others will recommend I make a new, one hundred per cent successful, attempt on my life in order to demonstrate beyond peradventure that I fully intended to carry out my original plan. If that is what you're thinking you can all go fuck yourselves. That's right – you can go take a running jump in the lake, because this is my body and this is my life.

Memo to self #1 – disband the Sandie Shaw Fan Club (SSFC) with immediate effect. Memo to self #2 – if, or when, he asks about the note, or its absence, tell Dad whatever he most wants to hear. Memo to self #3 – he/him, she/her, they/them.

To whom it may concern – the blood is no more. I can reveal that the blood is no longer present in Dad's semen. It vanished as mysteriously as it arrived. So, all those tests were for nothing. They didn't find any nasties, which is the best news I can share. Typical of Dad – in his diary he said he had undergone a urological MOT and could now forget about blood for a whole twelve months.

WHEN HE ASKS AT THE WHITTINGTON if he can see Henry briefly this morning instead of during visiting hours they tell him it is highly irregular – the doctors and interns will be doing their rounds very soon. Various occupied beds come and go through the double doors at the hands of porters and medics in scrubs. It strikes Donaldson he hasn't actually been in such a bed since the day he was born.

'I have an appointment later,' he tells his son, who leans against two pillows, wearing striped pyjamas, with a crêpe bandage around his head and headphones around his neck.

'At the hospital?' the boy asks immediately, as if he knows the answer to his question. 'I mean the other hospital. I assume it's not this one – that would be too much of a coincidence.'

'What do you know about all that?' Donaldson fires back.

'Just a hunch,' Henry says. 'I saw a letter on the doormat.'

'Nothing to worry about there,' Donaldson says, declining the offer of chocolate. 'Let's talk about you, shall we? We have twelve minutes, it seems.'

'That should be plenty,' Henry says. 'Didn't Mum tell you? I want to transition. Do you know what that means, Dad?'

'It means you want to transition from male to female.'

'That's right. That's exactly right.'

'Are you sure about all this?' Donaldson asks. What he means is something slightly different. What he means is – why would you kill yourself if you really want to go through with this thing? Again, he imagines his ignorance rides roughshod over instincts felt deeply by his son – impulses beyond the father's ability to understand. Or maybe his son never actually intended to kill himself. Was this a cry for help, so called? Once again, Donaldson dismisses that notion as unworthy of his son. Perhaps life itself bores Henry. Existence is not really for him. These scrambled thoughts crowd in on the father so that he scarcely knows how to act. 'Sorry – of course, you're sure. We'd better get on with it then, hadn't we? Please understand your mother and I will do everything we can to support you.'

'The only clinic – in Belsize Park – is closing its doors to people like me.'

'I'm sure other places will spring up soon.' He is all at sea here. He doesn't know how to help his son. 'Good places –' he says with a wild shot at conviction. 'Progressive places.'

'You don't mind? I mean, you don't –'

'Object? Jesus Christ – we love you, Henry. We don't want to lose you. Meaning we don't want to lose you all over again. Should I even call you that? Henry, I mean?'

'That's the name you gave me, isn't it? That's the name I plan to keep.'

'Oh. I guess as a name it's pretty much –'

'All purpose? It's pretty much all purpose?'

'If you say so, Henry. Smile for me, please.'

'Sure thing, Dad. Be happy for me, won't you?'

'What do you want for your sixteenth birthday?'

'Nothing. I just want to be able to ride my bike on the streets of London.'

He doesn't ask about the note – the absent note. It doesn't feel like the right thing to do. Perhaps there will be another time to talk about it, a better time. Can there ever be a better time, a right time, for such a thing? For Donaldson it is enough simply to keep going, to put one foot in front of the other, at this hour. Such a paucity of ambition unmans him today. It promises to bring him even lower tomorrow. In fact, he could hardly feel worse about himself than he does already, despite his wife's harsh verdict on him as self-satisfied and vain. In the upstairs seminar room at Queen Anne's he surveys a dwindling band of students together with a burgeoning number of vacant desks.

'Where's Melanie today?' he asks Siobhan with just a hint of resignation or defeat in his voice.

'Sorry, Don,' she says with a little disclaimer of a shrug. 'It must be something in the water.'

'Don't tell me –' he says. 'It's the curse of Angela Carter. Well, best of luck to both ladies.'

First Nathan, now Melanie. They are all falling by the wayside. They are dropping like flies. Soon he will be talking to himself in a room filled with ghosts. They are due to discuss sympathy and irony as competing or contrasting narrative methods, but Donaldson no longer has the stomach for it. He is thinking that maybe he will take a sabbatical, or a leave of absence, or whatever the principal wants to call it. He needs to step back and examine his life in the light of recent events and developments. He might hire a camper van and drive through the highlands of Scotland for three months. He might walk out one midsummer morning in the footsteps of Laurie Lee, traipsing from this end of Iberia to that until he finds his very own Spanish civil war on the glittering shores of the Mediterranean.

'Titles –' he says. 'We were discussing titles, were we not? And that is a good thing because your holiday homework – those of you who elect to eschew the late Angela Carter and her popular course – has everything to do with titles and their consequences.'

'The title can make or break a story,' Dylan says supportively. 'Some writers can't start working until they hit on a title for their novel or screenplay. Often, they don't even know what their story is going to be about at that point in time.'

'That's very true, Dylan,' the senior lecturer says, gathering his strength. 'Take Muriel Spark, for example. For five or six weeks she would pace up and down the living room of her flat in Kensington or Chelsea or wherever she happened to find herself, puffing away on cigarette after cigarette until it came to her as in a dream – the vital, the necessary, the indispensable title. Then it was all downhill. She would rattle off sixty or seventy thousand words in a torrent of fluency and facility. What's the point here? The point is I want you to write me a story which has the title *Under the Bridge at Midnight*.'

'Midnight Cowboy,' says Dylan, fast out of the blocks. 'No – Midnight Express.'

'*Midnight's Children*,' Siobhan says, following up. 'Or *Midnight in the Garden of Good and Evil.*'

'Midnight At The Oasis,' Reuben offers in his turn. 'Midnight Rambler, anyone? Or how about Midnight Train To Georgia? I rest my storytelling case right there.'

'Any length you like,' Donaldson says. Suddenly, he hears it. Oh, my goodness – the songbird is singing in the tree again. Can it be so? The senior lecturer has the crazy idea the bird is singing just for him. 'Poem, story or script –' he confirms. 'The choice is yours. Think of the distant past. Consider the far future. I don't care where you take me, as long as it's somewhere I've never been before.'

HE IS ACCELERATING AND BRAKING, stopping and restarting. On the North Circular Road the traffic is as bad as ever. And today the faithful Renault is not really itself. When Donaldson hits the gas the response from the old jalopy is disappointing. There is not much in the way of oomph. No doubt the engine is enfeebled – Donaldson ascribes this to old age entirely, as if the car is a venerable uncle or aunt obliged at last to accept a reduced level of mobility. But look – there it is. As he comes to a halt outside the hospital, Donaldson sees it – a little red dashboard light he has never seen before.

66

'We'd like to do some further tests,' says the urologist, a burly Pole with no sense of humour, from behind a large computer screen that creates an obvious and unwelcome barrier to understanding.

'Really?' Donaldson counters. 'I'm here to tell you the blood has gone. There is no blood –'

'Even so, we'd like to do some more tests.'

'But the blood has gone away of its own accord.' They want to do further tests. Are they perhaps being rewarded on a test-by-test basis? What about a full body scan in the tunnel? If they carry on searching, they will eventually find a tumour the size of a tennis ball inside his head, Donaldson tells himself. 'If you'd tried antibiotics at the start, we could have saved ourselves a lot of trouble.'

'We undertook certain tests because we felt you were anxious about the blood. We initiated our programme so as to eliminate the possibility of cancer based on your family history. We discussed all this with you. Just because we haven't found anything doesn't mean there's nothing there.'

'Ha, ha – are you familiar with the later work of Franz Kafka? Look here – I'm discharging myself from the programme. I'm super grateful for your attention in this matter, and now I'm going home.'

Finally, the finish is in sight. He is on the North Circular Road for the very last time. He is in the middle lane with a little red light glaring at him from the dash. Without warning the faithful Renault loses power completely. It gives up the ghost there and then in the middle lane of the A406 with a Wood Green exit sign in view. Now there is oily smoke inside the car. As the ancient Renault slows, the driver opens a window and hits the hazard lights button. All around him the horns are honking, but Donaldson can't hear them. Now he does a strange thing. He closes the window and slumps forward against the steering wheel. At this time his own horn is honking – it means very little to him because there is a perfect silence inside his head. Then it presents – a creeping paralysis that starts in a region below his heart and travels up through his chest. Is he dying? He must be dying. He sees the albatross fall from the sky. He sees the parachute descend towards a shimmering sea. He sees a young girl turn through the air – she is smiling and waving. Everything falls. Everyone is falling. And now Donaldson lets out a tremendous cry of pain and hunger. This is something between a roar and a howl. At the same time his torso starts to shudder. His breathing is hugely compromised by internal forces. Then he gets it – he isn't dying, he is only *sobbing*, albeit in an extreme and uncontrolled way. This goes on for about ten seconds, during which Donaldson rocks backwards and forwards robotically in his seat, banging his forehead against the steering wheel every now and again for good measure. Then it stops, or lessens. He is much better now. He is going to be just fine. When he consults the mirror he sees a white van stationed directly behind the car. This van has drawn up two or three yards behind the Renault, all lights blazing. What is happening here? Oh, I say – a man with a ruddy face is knocking on the window right beside Donaldson's head.

'Are you all right?' the man asks, once Donaldson manages to open the window.

'Of course,' Donaldson says. 'I just need to get this rust bucket off the road.'

'You don't look too clever,' the man says. 'You look like you've seen a ghost.'

'That's very possible,' Donaldson says. 'Can you tow me off the road or not?'

And now he is sitting inside the van. This takes place in north London. That's correct – he is actually sitting beside the white van man as together they navigate the back streets of heaven, or Wood Green.

'Recognised your number plate,' the man says. 'I'm good that way – with remembering stuff.'

'I'm very happy to hear that,' Donaldson says. 'It's just possible you saved my life back there.'

'Remember when I stole your car park space?' the man says. 'I'm sorry I done that to you –'

He is in his father's embrace. He is on a big Arab horse on an empty beach in France with his father's arm around him. They are riding hard in the liminal zone where the foam comes and goes on the strand. Up ahead in the distance is an abandoned lighthouse at low tide. To one side are the grasses and the dunes. To the other is the sea with, on it, three oil tankers come from Port Said. He is five or six, contented. He has the idea his father loves him. The hot sun.

ON THURSDAY, QUITE LATE in the day, he makes up his mind. He has had certain reservations with regard to the address, in respect of how to get hold of Nathan's address, but these doubts have since been resolved. He could have got the address from school records, but such a course of action falls firmly, he decides, into a category labelled bad form. He could have asked his students, but that would be a little creepy, wouldn't it? In any case, they would probably tell him to consult the school's records. No, this is the best way forward, Donaldson concludes as he buttons a plaid shirt and checks his look in the mirror. It is not the only way. It is the right way – the way it would happen in a book.

He is outside the pub in West Hampstead with the first lights coming on in the flats around him. When he crosses the threshold of the pub, or, rather, its annex, the die will be cast. Inside the pub there is no sign of Nathan. That is quite OK. That is to be expected, if the student is indeed alone tonight. As Donaldson makes his way anxiously towards the annex at the other end of a short corridor he hears the music begin. They are playing his song. They are playing Islands In The Stream. Inside the annex he hugs the wall while the dancers conduct their choreographed manoeuvres in rows of ten or twelve. In the end he doesn't have to do anything at all. It happens just the way he hoped it would. Nathan detaches himself from the matrix of activity and comes right over as if it is perfectly obvious, as if they had always intended to meet in this particular context and on this particular night. And for Donaldson, who has spent a great deal of time considering the rules of attraction and worrying about what to say first, the whole matter is made easy when Nathan Ford takes it out of his hands.

'Nice shirt, professor.'

'Thanks. I found it at the bottom of a drawer.'

'Looks fresh out of the box to me.'

'OK – so I bought it at Brent Cross last Saturday.'

'With me in mind?'

'Maybe.'

'That's cute. So, shall we hit the floor? I believe you know this one, don't you?'

'Wait – I wanted to ask you something. There's something I've been meaning to ask you.'

'Slow down, Don. Is it all right if I call you Don? I mean – is it still all right?'

'Would you like to do Scotland with me in a VW camper van?'

'Is that *Scotland* Scotland? And, if so, when do we start?'

To live is to dream. He feels good about himself. He feels good about his new shirt. He has done all the thinking. He is through with thinking and its various offshoots or subsidiaries. There is a taste in his mouth he doesn't recognise. It must be the taste of tomorrow, he decides – the savour of life, or truth. 'Look –' he says. 'I'm serious. I feel I could tell you anything and you wouldn't judge me. I mean you wouldn't hold it against me. Does that make sense?'

'Well, now – it certainly sounds serious. What about your wife and kids?'

'My wife and kids have made alternative holiday arrangements this year.'

'Oh. In that case I should probably tell you I don't know how to drive –'

They agree. They are agreed on most things. In the republic of north London the evening tightens its grip on idea and expectation. Outside in the streets the rain falls gently on the heads of strangers and lovers. This rain is OK. This is the rain that beads the petals of desert flowers with dewy droplets. A single-decker bus, very brightly lit up, is coming. They run for the bus.

My Benidorm Summer

THE FIRST THING TO SAY ABOUT MY MOTHER is that she was an alcoholic. She was other things too, of course, but it is by her sad and lonely drinking that she will always be defined in my memory and imagination. Look – I have barely begun, but already this feels like a confession. I must resist the temptation to hog all the blame – that would be greedy. In fact, it was no one's fault. Doubtless each life's story is a coming together of forces over which we have little influence or control. How else to account for the wretchedness of the average existence? As for my late mother's decline – let's admit right here it was an important staging post on my own descent into disappointment and disillusion. What happened back then – it was inevitable in many ways, wasn't it? That is what I choose to believe today. But is it enough to excuse me? Will it be sufficient to get me off the hook? Getting – or, more properly, *staying* – off the hook is the ultimate aspiration, it seems to me, in a base and selfish world.

In the long summer holiday before my last year at school my mother, who lived then in a dreary new town in Scotland, packed me off to Benidorm, where my father owned a successful restaurant below a twelve-storey hotel beside the sea. Both the restaurant and the hotel were popular with British tourists, of whom there were a great many in those days and in those parts. Benidorm has two very fine beaches – that is its misfortune. Set in a bay of one small island, and hot underfoot from noon until night, are the *playas levante* and *poniente* – so labelled because they catch the rising and setting suns respectively on nineteen days out of twenty during peak season. My father's diner was located pretty much in the middle of a garish strip of karaoke bars, greasy spoons, tattoo parlours and souvenir shops, many fielding the colours of the union flag in some shape or form, that lined the more easterly of these two beaches. All-day breakfasts were the speciality of the house. It goes without saying that fish and chips, plus all manner of culinary derivatives featuring foodstuffs in batter, were very popular at Fast Freddie's Diner, regardless of the hour. My father, who set the prevailing standard of service but who was no longer active at the grill, was a decent cook by any measure. I do want to be fair to my father in all of this. That is very important to me. If this is to be a British tale, driven by trademark arrogance and false modesty operating together in restive harmony, it should at least be *fair* to all concerned.

At this time my mother worked at a Timpson shoe outlet in the sprawling shopping mall designed by well-intentioned planners and architects to be the living, breathing heart of a vibrant community. That she had come to this condition of employment was a source of fierce pride to my mother, who was a snob in the nicest sense of the word. She, who had a clear-sighted duty to sponsor the personal improvement of others, was obliged to park her own contentment somewhere obscure on the hard shoulder of later life. Principally to blame for this state of affairs were a bitter divorce from my father, which left her isolated from the current of lived experience, and an unfavourable financial settlement from which she never recovered. Married at all times to these basic circumstances was my mother's alcoholism. Did her drinking fuel the split, you might reasonably ask, or was it the other way round? Chicken or egg – which came first? I don't think it makes any useful difference, does it?

Three days a week after school it was my custom to meet my mother, by that hour released from her shoe boxes, at a purpose-built public house with neither atmosphere nor character but with telephone kiosk and bus stop stationed helpfully outside it – this at the outer limits of our charmless town centre. For a son to meet his alcoholic mother in a desolate bar at the edge of our town no doubt strikes you as perverse, or at best foolish. I venture to disagree. To see her sitting at her usual table, defiantly alone in a fake fur jacket, lipstick on and hair piled up on top of her head, made me cry out inside. She was waiting for me – only for me. After she gave me the money I went up to the bar and bought the drinks. I always drank a half pint of beer – special or heavy – although I would rather have had a Coke or a Pepsi or something else. I think she understood this instinctively. First, she gave my hand a small squeeze of sympathy or complicity. Then she took a little sip of her brandy and soda, the drinker's drink *par excellence*, before wiping the red lipstick from the rim of her glass with a tissue and settling back to look at me. It was more or less the same every time we met like this. My role was to indulge her. I would permit her to flatter me, the only man in her life, for as long as it took her to finish her drink. It should have been sordid or seedy, but it wasn't. It was actually moving to me and my anxious way of thinking. It was during these difficult moments that I came to know how much my mother loved me and how much she hated herself, or what she had become. Looking back now it is these hard-won truths that I rely on to help me make sense of my life.

'What was it this time?' she asked today, as she always did.

'Piano,' I told her, as I had often done before. These additional classes after school proper were my mother's way of screwing a little extra funding out of my father. That there was no material benefit to her didn't matter. What counted was the mere fact of the classes. It didn't even matter that I had no real talent for the piano or music. 'Wednesday is photography,' I said. 'I think you know that, don't you? And on Friday I have Spanish. I honestly don't know what to expect this week. It sounds corny or crazy, but last week I was saved by the bell. My teacher made a pass at me —'

'Ah —' she said, cupping her glass with both hands as if to warm them, and nodding at the centre of the table where my second-hand Pentax gleamed dully in the company of four sorry beer mats. 'I'm really not surprised to hear that, dear.'

What could she mean? Either it came as no surprise to her that such things went on in the world, or it failed to surprise her that such things happened to me. I decided not to let on. I decided not to tell my mother that my Spanish teacher was an *hombre*, a man. In any case she had probably already worked all that out for herself. And what good would it do anybody anyway? I had always taken it for granted that one interested party or another would feel me up, or try to, when the opportunity presented itself. 'Did I tell you I came first in French?' I said instead.

'No,' she said. 'I'm very proud of you, Keith. You know that, don't you? You mean the whole lousy world to me.' At this juncture she always looked me straight in the eye before suggesting it. 'Aren't we going to have one more drink for the road — just a tiny one?'

'I don't think so,' I said in line with established ritual. 'Did you get a letter from Dad this morning?' I had seen it on the doormat, a blueish air mail envelope stamped exotically and addressed in my father's excellent hand. It was well known she had taught him how to write like that as part of her schedule of improvements. 'How is he?' I asked. 'He never writes to me now. I guess I must embarrass him somehow, or displease him generally. Either that or he's much too busy folding napkins and shelling prawns.'

'He wants you to go to Spain. I mean for the whole summer. Shall I say no, darling? Should I tell him you'd rather stay here with me?' There it was. Her tone and disposition had altered very subtly, as they always did at this stage, and I understood it was time to go home. 'Don't worry,' she went on. 'It's all arranged with the money and the flights. Oh – and he makes a real point of this. Your father insists you pass a scooter or motorbike test without delay.'

I didn't intend to pop the question. This notion of my parents assembled in the same hotel lobby as each other while some unseen jukebox played a fatuous hit record was beyond comprehension, or beyond reason. 'Will you come too?' I asked my mother anyway, even as I processed first the casual hurt and then, immediately after, the longer-term pain associated with this wild request.

'I don't think so,' she said brightly, draining her glass for the third or fourth time. 'Give me Puerto Pollensa any day of the week. And you wouldn't want to be with me any more than you absolutely *had* to, would you, darling? No, don't answer that question, please. It isn't fair on you –'

'Puerto Pollensa?' I came back loyally, rolling the lovely words around on my tongue while dragging my school bag towards me under the table. 'I don't even know where that is.' To me the place sounded like the type of boardwalk hangout favoured by desperate men bent on dividing up the loot as the law closed in on them. No, it was the inspiration for a new perfume, surely – an unforgettable fragrance to evoke a special moment in time.

'Maybe you'll take me there one day,' she argued humorously, as if she had in mind a coral island in the south Pacific or a lesser moon of Jupiter. 'Meanwhile,' she added, 'please just promise you'll call me once a week from Spain. Hang the expense, I say. You do know how to raid a till, don't you? I always believed that Swiss army knife your father gave you would come in handy one day.'

I wasn't thinking about raiding any tills. In fact, I was thinking about going up in a jet plane for the first time in my life. Yes, that's how untravelled I was at sixteen. I was thinking about going up in a big silver bird, plus a host of other things besides. If you asked me to locate the starting point for my signature guilt across the decades, I wouldn't hesitate to tell you – it began right there in that dreadful bar. The truth is I was busy thinking about sun, sea, sand, and how I might lose my virginity, still technically intact at that time. In this last regard Benidorm presented itself as a place of limitless potential – I made a mental note on the spot to consider the idea of travelling *prepared*, as in purchasing such accessories as might be required for the trip. From the pavement opposite the pub I took a picture of my mother, her hands raised in protest, with the flagship phone box on one side and the iconic bus shelter on the other. This last likeness ever made of her – a black and white shot of no particular aesthetic distinction – has the force today of a vital piece of forensic evidence. I love that photograph. It means the whole lousy world to me.

I TOOK THE SLEEPER FROM EDINBURGH to London, and then – at considerable expense – a black cab to the airport. There wasn't time for bacon and eggs, sunny side up or any other way. I was obliged to confront on an empty stomach the prospect of my first ever flight, which turned out to be a good thing. I didn't have to wait until we reached our cruising height of 36,000 feet, or anywhere close to it, in order to feel queasy. In fact, I began to puke very soon after we cleared the roofs of the houses at the end of the runway. This was in the halcyon days, if they ever existed, of air travel. Back then, the armrest beside you contained a tiny metal ashtray, quickly filled to capacity, while the elasticated seat pocket in front of you housed a deftly scripted menu with a timetable for mid-air refreshments, plus – absurdly and crucially – a paper sick bag. It looks like no one gets sick in jet planes any more, which must, I suppose, be viewed as a type of progress. On first taking to the skies, however, I found that waxy paper bag to have life-saving properties. Equally comforting were the sick bags on either side of me. I had the middle seat in a row of three towards the front of the cabin. To my right at the oval window was a dark-skinned boy about my age with a precociously sensual air, rather long eye lashes, and the first hints of a moustache above his cruel mouth. On my left at the aisle was a young woman, a few years older than me, with straight black hair and a fresh, floral scent that made a sensory mockery of my feeble retching. We were somewhere above the Pyrenees when I plucked up the courage to engage with my sweet-smelling neighbour using the ideal excuse.

'Do you mind if I borrow your sick bag?' I began. 'Mine seems to be nearly full, and we still have a long way to go by my reckoning. Just an insurance policy, really. I'd hate to spring a leak –'

'Be my guest,' she said, laughing and raising her table for long enough to find what she was looking for. 'Just don't give it back to me afterwards, if you don't mind.'

'It must be because I haven't eaten,' I suggested gamely. 'But, you know, I don't actually feel the slightest bit hungry.'

'Don't worry,' she said confidentially. 'It has nothing to do with eating or not eating. It's simply a question of altitude. You started retching two minutes after we took off from London and you'll stop exactly two minutes before we touch down at Alicante.'

'Are you a nurse?' I asked, impressed. 'Or an aviation industry insider, perhaps, on a fact-finding mission?'

'I'm neither of those things,' she said, closing her book on the little table and parking her hands there with a clinking of bracelets. She was Spanish, wasn't she? Yet she spoke perfect English with no trace of a foreign accent. As for her paperback novel – although it was turned face down modestly in front of her, we could tell, those of us who were interested, that it was something weighty or classic in English. 'If you went up a mountain in a car,' she explained with her easy-going authority, 'the same thing would surely happen. It's all about height above sea level.' She wasn't, even at this late stage, quite finished with my case or my condition. 'Most young people,' she disclosed, smiling just enough and not too much, 'grow out of the whole thing at puberty.'

Oh, Isabella – did you have any idea how clever you appeared to that unworldly schoolboy with a sick bag in his hand? Naturally, you did. There was nothing you didn't know. There was nothing you couldn't see. Relative height above sea level – this was only one of your specialisms in life. That you chose to sit at a one-seat remove from your brother was merely confirmation, if any were needed, of your qualities. Kids, everyone agrees, must have the window. It is to the aisle that grown-ups are mostly drawn. Of course, Manolito was hardly a *kid*, as such, was he? Every now and then – but far too often, I judged, to be an accident – he rubbed his leg against mine in the dangerous valley that stretches left or right below the folding tables and the in-flight magazines. You probably saw that too.

We were at the carousel in the arrivals hangar, waiting for our luggage to appear on the belt. Isabella's valise – the word had been invented for her exclusive use, I imagined – glided effortlessly into view, with Manolito's suitcase not far behind. I felt more and more sure of it – these were privileged, exceptional people. Their baggage always arrived shortly before everyone else's.

'Oh, well –' the sister said, frowning politely while her brother winked at me over her shoulder. 'I guess this is goodbye, Keith. We wish you an enjoyable stay here in Alicante, don't we, Manolito?'

'We certainly do, Isabella. It's a charming city with a great deal to offer the discerning visitor.'

'You're very kind,' I said. 'But the fact is I'm not staying here in Alicante. My final destination is Benidorm. Sorry to disappoint, and all that. Looks like a one-hour coach journey for me now.'

'Oh, you poor thing,' Isabella attested as I rescued my suitcase with some minor input at close range from her brother. 'You simply must come along with us as far as Benidorm. We insist on it, don't we, Manolito?'

'One hundred per cent. No question about it. In fact, we won't take no for an answer, Keith.'

'Why didn't you mention Benidorm earlier, for heaven's sake? Now, we really have to find you a *bocadillo,* or a *jamón* sandwich, this instant. Look – *pesetas.* You must be dying of hunger –'

He was waiting calmly for us outside the terminal building in the scrum of taxis and buses. This was our chauffeur, a much older man of infinite discretion, dressed all in white. As for our transport – a massive American number with white-wall tyres, tail fins, and bench seats – it was pitched somewhere between car and limousine. I was in a hot dream. The entire planet basked in the midday sun.

'Why don't you sit up front with Paco?' Isabella suggested as a cavernous boot, or trunk, devoured our suitcases. This, it struck me, was less an invitation than a directive. Could it be the clever sister was conspiring to separate, for their own comfort and safety, guest from brother? 'You'll get a better view of the countryside that way. Enjoy it while you can. As soon as we hit Benidorm you'll forget all about the countryside as a meaningful concept. It never existed –'

She was right about the view, just as she was right about all the rest. For the best part of an hour we swept imperiously through a landscape dotted with orange groves and sloping vineyards backed by rugged sierras that sucked the cloud from the surrounding sky. I was in the cockpit. I was in pole position. Every so often we caught a glimpse of the shining sea – it kept its distance at first, then seemed to draw us rapidly closer as we neared journey's end. No one spoke. Not a word was spoken on that stately and surrealistic dash across south-east Spain. What was it? Valencia province? I didn't know. I didn't ask. From time to time a strange idea occurred to me. I was being kidnapped by a sibling team of hoodlums intent on extracting a tidy sum in ransom money from my father, the celebrated English restaurateur. Who were these people, and what did they want with me? If I had a chance to find out there and then, I didn't take it. Suddenly, the city was before us – no, magically *below* us. It took the form of a densely-packed crescent of high-rise hotels and apartment blocks that hugged the shoreline beyond a dusty no man's land of farmyards, fields and fincas. I don't know why. I didn't understand why I should feel immediately at home here. It was just a sensation I had as our car left the highway and descended smoothly towards the strip, or the centre of town. Then she was leaning forward from behind, and it was as if someone had clicked their fingers in my ear.

'Where would you like Paco to set you down, Keith?' she asked. 'As you can see, it's quite a big place.'

'It's a very big place,' I said, snapping out of my reverie. 'I'm not absolutely sure where I want to get out, to be quite frank with you.' This was sheer nonsense, but I didn't care. OK – I did care. The truth is I was inexplicably ashamed of who I was at that precise moment in time. The truth is I didn't want these people to drop me off within a mile of Fast Freddie's Diner. That's it – I felt ashamed of my family, my roots, my life, the whole deal. Then I felt doubly ashamed of myself for being ashamed in the first place. This feeling was something new to me – no doubt I found it disorientating and distressing as I entered uncharted waters. 'Pretty much anywhere on the strip will do nicely, I dare say. Preferably on the Levante side of town, I guess – if it's not too much trouble.'

'It's not too much trouble at all,' Isabella said before she rattled something off to Paco.

'Are you sure you'll be all right, Keith?' the brother chipped in. 'Don't you have an address to go to?'

Of course, I had an address. I had exhaustive directions, too – these were safely tucked away in my wallet, together with a sketch map my father had drawn for me, and two hundred quid in cash and travellers' cheques (less the taxi fare from this morning). As the car pulled powerfully away it left me standing on a busy pavement with my suitcase in my hand and my heart in my mouth. It was just a feeling I had, based on an inkling or a premonition or something like that. The overhead sun was no comfort. The sea breeze offered no consolation. When I reached behind me finally I discovered my hunch of five seconds ago was correct. Immediately, I felt faint, and a sweat broke out under my T-shirt. My crowded, necessary wallet was no longer a part of me. In my hip pocket there was no longer a billfold matching that, or any other, description. First, I panicked. Then I toyed with the idea, before rejecting it angrily, of bursting into tears and demanding to meet with a relevant authority. When I played back the tape of my long day it was painfully obvious what had befallen me. That it was blindingly obvious only made it harder to accept. I had no evidence and no facts – *nada*. I had made a false start here in Benidorm – this much was plain. It was a catastrophic reversal. How could I have imagined I *liked* this tawdry town? And yet there was no going back from where I stood – that was the long and the short of it. I had to face the music. It would be a test of my character – I had few doubts in that regard. Suddenly, the suitcase in my hand felt reassuring. The sun was my new ally. Right away I set about asking for directions in Spanish to my father's restaurant.

Within a few minutes I was standing diagonally opposite Fast Freddie's Diner with the sun on my neck and the beach at my back. Gazing up at the hotel I got to wondering whether my room would have a balcony with a decent view. I almost laughed at this absurd distraction – it acted on behalf of an intrinsic improbability. Funny what heart and head conjure up when the chips are down. I needed to decide on my plan. I had to get my story straight right now. After I crossed the road it would be too late. Outside the diner the air was redolent of fried food – of onion rings, say. All the pavement tables were taken. There was a lot of cigarette smoke. A youngish woman wearing a short, tight skirt clip-clopped towards me purposefully, a notepad tucked into her belt.

'*Hola*,' she said. 'I'm Barbara. Are you hungry, or lost, or both? Ah, yes – you're *Keith*, right?'

BARBARA WAS DAD'S GIRLFRIEND. At first, I thought of her rather uncharitably as his lover or his mistress – this last designation was a technical impossibility, of course, thanks to his divorced status. In short order, however, I came to view Barbara in a more positive light. That is because she was all right. She even offered to take my suitcase from me during those first few awkward moments on the pavement, as if she thought it might be too heavy for me, or too heavy *under the present circumstances*. I had a choice here. I could either conclude she judged me weak, or I could decide she was extending the hand of friendship. Like I say – Barbara was all right. As she led me up the four flights of stairs to a room on the second floor of the hotel she told me my father was out of town for the day.

'Oh,' I said, locating the humble but meaningful word midway between disappointment and relief. Why relief? I still had no fixed idea of how to account for my missing wallet – or, rather, the absent funds associated with it. Perhaps I imagined I could just say nothing about anything, and everything would be all right. If so, I was dead wrong. 'I guess he must have forgotten I was arriving today.'

'Not at all,' Barbara said. 'I have a feeling he had to act quickly on something. I mean at short notice. A business opportunity, most probably. There are plans afoot, Keith – *plans*.'

'Oh?' I said again. 'Plans for what, exactly?'

'You'll see. All in good time. Actually, I think everything is still at an early stage.' We were in a small, stuffy room – a single room with curtains drawn and an ancient AC poking through the wall from outside at high level. 'No sea view, I'm afraid,' Barbara said with a hint of genuine apology in her voice, opening the curtains to reveal the brick façade of the neighbouring block across a noisy side street. 'But what do you expect for the money?' she went on, casting around for a switch. 'It's dog eat dog in this dirty town.' Here, she gave me a rueful smile as the air conditioner started up reluctantly above her head. 'Your father said he'd sent you the money – or a cheque, or something – in advance. Is that right, Keith?'

It transpired that Barbara had some administrative job at the hotel, in addition to her role at Fast Freddie's, where it seemed to me she was stationed somewhere between manager and *maîtresse d*. If anything, this assessment understated her influence and reach. It soon became obvious my father saw her as pretty much *everything* up to and including the rank of business partner. We were in the vast kitchen at the rear of the diner, where a new pizza oven was being installed within a kind of chimney breast made of stones. For two hours Barbara had kept me busy wiping menus, filling sauce bottles, stocking several freezers with bags of ice and chips, and, yes, folding napkins. Peeling prawns would no doubt come later. Now we were entering a different phase. Soon it would be time to face the music.

'Pizza is the future,' my father declared evangelically, patting the shoulder of an old tradesman he evidently knew personally as the stone oven took further shape in front of us. 'Pizza is where the smart money is, Keith.'

'Pizza and coffee,' Barbara confirmed soberly. 'Only, it's really too hot for coffee here, isn't it?'

'In July or August, perhaps,' my father allowed, presumably for my benefit. I had the feeling they had talked all this through a dozen times. 'The trick is to blur the seasons,' he went on, warming to his theme. 'Let's abolish summer and winter —'

'The challenge,' Barbara said, 'is to take our offer up market.'

The plan was to open a second restaurant, and then a third, using an altered appeal to the dining public based on the galloping fashion for pizza. Fish and chips — these were classic constituents, of course. On the other hand, it was important to move with the times. These market insights were released to me via regular briefings as my Benidorm summer unfolded. From day one, however, I had an unwelcome sense that my own future was somehow yoked, or about to be yoked, to my father's business ambitions. This feeling began there and then, before the first pizza oven had even been built.

'Dad —' I said now, cutting across the conversation. 'Do you mind if I speak to you alone? There's something I've been wanting to get off my chest.'

'No secrets here,' my father said, lighting another cigarette. He was always sparking up, or stubbing out, a cigarette. I don't think I ever saw him without a Rothmans King Size in either his mouth or his hand – at least, that's the way is seemed. 'Barbara already knows everything there is to know.'

'That's OK,' Barbara said amiably. 'I'd better get myself out there before the six o'clock horde descends on us, ravenous –'

For hours I had weighed up the pros and cons, or the ups and downs, of the affair. The whole thing went back to the arrivals hall at Alicante airport. My oh my – had it only been half a day ago? It felt more like half a lifetime. Manolito was pressing up against me as I rescued my suitcase from the carousel. This was a brief episode – I thought little of it at the time. Rather, I was focused on changing some money in order to buy a coach ticket to Benidorm. Funny – in the instant I was thinking about my wallet Monolito was actively engaged in stealing it. I gave no mind to the older sister here. Surely Isabella, with her bracelets and books, played no part in this. It was what came next that I couldn't accept. The idea that the boy would encourage me to complete my journey in *that* car, knowing I might discover the loss of my wallet from one minute to the next – it was brazen beyond belief. What did that say about him? What did it say about me? If I accused him, would he simply have denied it? What would have happened after that? If I told you I was almost *glad* I hadn't known, would you believe me? It made things easier, did it not? Life is so much more tolerable without confrontation. It made things a lot easier *then*. But right now I was facing one of life's game-changing decisions. Actions have consequences, don't they? That is fine by me. That is as it should be. Certain decisions, however, have ramifications that dog you forever. Why didn't I just tell the truth – not the whole truth necessarily, but a slimmed-down version of it? I had been pickpocketed at the airport. It was unfortunate, but it wasn't the end of the world. Yes, it made me look weak, and no son wants to look weak in front of his father. I had a choice to make, and I made it. For hours I had weighed up the merits and demerits of this or that course of action. And now the moment – I won't say *of truth* – had arrived.

'I'm very sorry, Dad,' I said. 'I can't pay for my room with the money you sent because I don't actually have it any more.'

'What happened?' my father asked me. He wasn't angry at this point – just perplexed. 'Did you lose it at the blackjack table or the roulette wheel?'

'Not exactly. I left the money in an envelope for Mum because she needs it more than me.'

I should have known this short exchange – straightforward in its essentials – would come back to bite me in some shape or form. Even at the time, the words had a scripted quality, as if they were lines in a play. All the while I worked flat out to convince myself I was doing the right thing. It was for her I did it – that's really all I can say. I want to give due credit here to my father – he resisted the idea of linking the missing money to my mother's drinking in any way. That would have been, by any reasonable standard, cheap – something he tried hard not to be.

There was nothing else for it. I said I would work longer hours to make up the shortfall, and I did. In the mornings you might find me washing gravy pots, or scraping the griddles, or scrubbing the extractors above the grills, or chopping up salad vegetables. In the afternoons I waited tables – I had responsibility for twenty covers below the striped awnings that faced the sea. At all times I operated under the watchful eye of Barbara. She had a soft spot for me – I felt this keenly, if in an obscure way. I think there was a maternal instinct buried deep inside Barbara – it struggled to get out. Perhaps she cast herself as the other woman in a role as old as history. At all events, she never rebuked me when I dropped a plate or forgot an order, and I was grateful to her for that. Barbara was OK – I really believed that at first.

In the warm evenings I was free. I was relatively free. From six o'clock until eleven I criss-crossed the city on my scooter, delivering take-out suppers to the hungry residents of Benidorm. It wasn't just me, of course. There was another delivery boy, Javier, who had a bad stammer, and who was naturally wary of me as the boss man's son. I never gave up on Javier. His English was only just better than my Spanish. We struck up a surly bond based on grunts exchanged through visors peppered with dead insects.

I felt free. It sounds crazy, I know – in many ways this was the best summer of my life. I had my map of the city and my aromatic food parcels – within a short space of time these parcels were traded for cardboard pizza boxes. Turned out my father was right – pizza *was* the future. It flew off the shelves. It sold like hot cakes. Soon I was at the centre of a thriving enterprise, an expanding empire of fast food. People liked me – that was the thing that caught me off guard. They ordered more and more product crowned with more and more outlandish ingredients. As the weeks went by, I came to know all my regular customers, distinguished as they were by a full gamut of foibles and eccentricities. There was pathos and there was bathos. A delivery boy clocks all humanity from the corner of one eye. Weekends, towards the top of a high-rise block of flats set back half a mile from the beach, the door was invariably opened by the same lonely misfit, a Mr Salvadori, with opportunistic erection held barely in check and a harmless allusion to extra salami. That these imperfect strangers warmed to me meant everything. It wasn't just pizza I brought them in the heat of the night. I was part of a vital growth industry. I was delivering dreams.

Each Sunday night at the same hour I called my mother from a booth on the promenade just a stone's throw from the sheltering sea. Each time it was the same thing. My heart sank immediately she answered. She was always completely drunk, and barely able to speak, so that I began to wonder whether she still had a job to go to. She would repeat my name over and over again, but with long pauses in between. It was always the same. I told her I loved her. I told her I would phone her at the same time next weekend. Then I hung up gently and went back to Fast Freddie's, where Barbara was waiting for me with a stack of pizza boxes in her arms. She knew – I could tell. Dad was right – she saw everything and she understood everything. I quickly came to dread those Sunday nights featuring a lonely call box overlooking the sea. The truth is I have never been a fan of Sunday night. Some ghosts stalk the imagination early, and you spend your whole life trying to get away from them.

PART SECOND
The Transgressive Tendency

MY BENIDORM SUMMER HAD THREE phases, independent but also overlapping. During the first phase I was largely innocent, ignorant, and happy (except on Sunday nights). Things didn't really fall apart until the third and final chapter. It was during the awkward central period, however, that the seeds of my downfall were sown. Every story has a beginning, middle and end. In life as in art, the second act is often host to a transgressive tendency – it is on this regrettable slippage, inevitably, that poor outcomes rely for their reach. Here, it began – or began again – with the big Oldsmobile. The great car, with its tail fins and white-wall tyres, was a harbinger of something malign. As it cruised past my busy tables on the strip, an inscrutable Paco at the wheel, the sleek machine took my breath away. There could be no doubting the significance of this intervention. It was all too clear to me. In that shocking moment the next phase of my life was inaugurated under the grinning sun.

One July evening I was summoned to a rambling finca located about a mile and a half from the beach on the dusty plain between city and coastal highway. I was aware that this remote destination would normally be on Javier's rounds – my fellow delivery boy was off sick that night. In the pink glow of the hour the Casa Hermosa was indeed a fine sight, partially visible above a high wall that bore *perros periculosos*, or beware of the dog, signs at regular intervals along its forbidding length. And there it was, right on cue, as I turned my engine off at the iron gates – a distant barking of two or more dogs raised on raw meat and deprived of affection. As I approached the buzzer with three pizza boxes in hand I was met with an instruction in a man's voice in Spanish. I was to remove my helmet. There was a pause now – it struck me that my presence at the gates in place of Javier must be the cause of this delay. Soon they swung open – the iron gates swung open noiselessly to reveal a driveway of tiny stones leading to the heavily shuttered house. Just as I decided to make my way on foot towards a brightly lit porch there came a female voice instructing me in English to bring my scooter inside the grounds. There was a clue there, wasn't there? There was a clue there in the use of the English language, but I failed to recognise it for what it was. Now the gates swung closed behind me and there was only the barking of the dogs growing somehow fainter, and the crunching of the stones beneath my feet. It was a magnificent place – a place of towering trees whose names I didn't know, of monumental shrubs with delicate flowers and six-inch spikes, and of delirious birdsong. At this time the airborne insects were at their most abundant, and the birds were swooping all around me in a frantic bid to empty the sky. It was lovely. Up ahead I glimpsed the car. The big blue sedan was stationed, its boot yawning negligently, a short distance from the porch. A sweat broke out as I stopped in my tracks, three boxes in my arms. The birds no longer swooped and sang. Should I have turned back in that moment? The gates were shut, and I valued my job. I thought about a stolen wallet – of course, I did. That wallet was still the focus of, or the vehicle for, a resentment directed at the universe in general and at Manolito in particular. Suddenly, it was too late for everything. The door to the house opened, and Isabella stood a few yards in front of me dressed all in turquoise linen and bathed in the amber light of the porch.

'Which one,' she began, 'is the more handsome of our couriers, I wonder? Javier or Keith?'

'Handsome is as handsome does,' I pointed out. 'That's why I brought you these irrefutable boxes of stout cardboard emblazoned with a leading brand name – ours. Nice boxes. Existential boxes –'

'You British –' she came back. 'You don't know how to accept a compliment.' Here on home ground she was extravagantly at ease with herself. She was even more at ease than she was on a jet plane or at an airport. The world, with all its sins and secrets, was hers to command. She might make it turn faster, or slower, according to whim or caprice. It was as if she had known all along this meeting would take place. But how could she have known? 'One day I must teach you,' she concluded, laughing in her light, teasing manner.

'Teach me what?'

'How to accept a compliment, of course.'

'Does it take long to learn?' I said, shuffling my boxes. 'Because I'm actually a very busy pizza delivery boy these days. Who knows? I may even make a career of it. There we are – one for Isabella, one for Manolito, and a third for somebody else. But not Paco, I don't think. He doesn't strike me as the type.'

'Wait here, please,' she said. 'I just want to check the order is complete. Wouldn't it be a pity if you had to come all the way back here for some reason? I don't know what I'd do if that happened.'

Then she turned and disappeared into a gloomy interior which receded room by room and which had a brightly illuminated space – a kitchen, no doubt – towards the rear. I don't know why I did it. I don't know why I crossed that threshold without being invited to. Let's just say it was totally out of character. I was in a large hallway, or a vestibule, which housed a great many stuffed beasts of all types and sizes and which was lashed by slim shadows, including my own, thrown horizontally by the lamps of the porch behind me. It should have been grotesque or unsettling. It wasn't. In fact, the effect was oddly comforting. It was also poignant and affecting, like a telegram sent from the front line or from the bridge of a sinking ship. I found some enchantment in this bizarre setting. Here, in the company of a gazelle and a leopard and a peacock and an upright bear, I forgot who I was and what I struggled to be. Then I saw the bigger picture – I was adrift in a room full of floor-to-ceiling mirrors. Just as I was about to back away from this fairground attraction I sensed a slight agitation, a small infelicity in the interplay of shadows, somewhere towards the back of the space. Immediately, I understood what was happening. I didn't have to think about it. It was as if all feeling and sense and perception were automatically enhanced, or accelerated, in this special environment. The air was thicker – no, *richer* – here.

'Do you like our little menagerie, Keith? Our father was a keen hunter and collector.' As he spoke, Manolito stepped forward, as if to declare himself more physically within a psychic landscape. 'I'd turn on the electric light right now,' he continued, 'but I don't want to startle you.'

'Turn it on, by all means,' I said. 'I won't mind a bit. I'm really not that easily startled. As a matter of fact, I could happily stumble around in here all night if I didn't have better things to do.'

'Do I detect some anger in you, Keith? Am I getting just a little hostility from you this evening?'

I was determined not to give ground. Even though I felt myself somehow tricked, or hoodwinked, I was resolved not to concede an inch of territory. As for the business of the stolen wallet – I had only recently consigned it to the history book. It was part of my past, not my future. Just to mention it now would be a social step backwards, a type of political gaffe. 'I should probably wait outside,' I said. 'The air is cool, finally, and the light is perfect. Are you familiar with the concept of the gloaming, Manolito? It's a Scottish term to describe a particular quality of daylight. An ideal quality –'

'An ideal quality, indeed,' Manolito said. 'You know – I think we could apply that self-same notion, or definition, without undue difficulty, to you, Keith. Don't be afraid of us, please. You mustn't be. Isabella and I – we like you very much.'

There was no time to react to, or reflect on, these calculated and calculating insights. I didn't see her arrive. I hadn't heard her footsteps. She must have been gliding on the air. Suddenly, the light came on in the mirrored hall and she was standing beside Manolito. 'What fascinating things are you two boys dreaming up here in the dark?' she asked, taking her brother's hand in hers.

They did everything together. They acted always in concert. They were of one mind. Late that night, as I lay on my narrow bed in my lonely hotel room, I began to wonder about the third pizza. I started to think about who it was for. If it wasn't intended for Paco, who was it meant for? Then I tried to recall which pizzas they had ordered in the first place. That I, an experienced pizza delivery boy, couldn't actually remember their order struck me as absurd – no, dangerous. It struck me as dangerous, somehow, but I couldn't tell you why. Then the whole idea of linking pizzas of any description with danger or jeopardy struck me as *beyond* absurd. These people had got to me in ways I didn't understand. It must have been after midnight when I tried to put the whole fantastic episode behind me. The overhead light in my room still burned. As I rose from the bed to lock my door someone knocked on it softly.

'Who is it?' I called out from the middle of the room.

'It's me – Barbara. Can I come in, please, Keith?'

'Come in,' I said. 'I don't think the door's locked.'

I had some clothes on, but not many. We lay down beside one another on the divan, and I asked her about a bruise below her eye. She told me she had banged into a door. Then she started crying. I told her I had seen my father behave violently towards my mother on two occasions – once when I was just a child, and once when I was a little older, in another room in a different place. I had never seen my father actually hit my mother. Was he capable of striking a woman, a woman like Barbara?

'Oh, but that sounds awful,' she said now, pulling a crumpled tissue from the sleeve of her cardigan. 'You poor thing –'

'They didn't know I was there,' I said. 'They didn't know I was watching them.'

'Of course not,' she said, breathing in deeply. 'Have you ever brought it up since?'

'Not until tonight,' I said. 'I don't think there's ever a good time to bring something like that up, is there?'

'Don't worry,' she said. 'It's not your fault. You mustn't blame yourself, Keith. That's what the children end up doing, you know. They carry it with them –'

There was a long silence during which I got to thinking about Barbara. I mean I started thinking about her as a young girl with a pony tail and wide apart eyes. What secrets lay behind those eyes? Were they good secrets or ugly secrets? 'Are you all right?' I asked her at last. We were lying side by side, arms crossed over our chests, looking up at a dripping AC. 'You can stop here tonight if you like. I'm going to roll over now and go to sleep.'

'Don't you find me attractive?' she asked, not quite out of the blue. 'I mean – don't you find me desirable?'

'Yes,' I told her after a short, but always reasonable, delay.

'How old are you?' she asked. 'That's the sixty-four-thousand-dollar question, isn't it? I can't believe I'm even asking you that.'

'I'm old enough,' I said somewhat primly, 'to fight and die for my country. But you already knew that, didn't you?'

'Don't you want me?' she enquired sadly, tucking her tissue away again.

'I probably wouldn't know where to begin,' I admitted.

'Would you like me to teach you?' she said. 'I can be a pretty good teacher, Keith –'

Everyone wanted to teach me. I was everyone's favourite pupil that summer in Benidorm. When I finally fell asleep I was thinking about my mother, and how I was going to help her quit drinking. I was thinking about my father, and how I was going to challenge him with my version of the past. I fell asleep that night with my face to the wall and my heart full of guilt and shame. The truth is I felt powerless to do anything to, or for, anyone. I was a coward of sorts. I didn't have what was needed to be the kind of man I wanted to be. When I asked myself what that kind might be I couldn't give myself a straight answer. A brave man, perhaps? A holy one? An explorer, maybe? No – a poet, surely. If only I'd known my true vocation was regret – I would have slept much easier that night and saved myself a lot of pointless soul searching. And now there was Barbara, fitfully asleep and facing away from me on my narrow bunk. It was obvious to me even then that she would come to resent me for what we had just done. We slept with the main light on and the noise of the AC coming and going in our dreams. When I woke up later I was alone.

I DIDN'T CONFRONT MY FATHER – not immediately. I chose not to challenge him, at least not in a direct way, on the subject of the past.

Instead, I consigned my feelings once again to a metal trunk in the attic of my imagination and slammed the lid shut. Here, in a dusty domain of leering rocking horses and warping tennis racquets, my secrets were spared the harsh verdict of a spiteful world.

There was just him and me. Barbara had gone away – I didn't know where, and I didn't know for how long. How long does it take for a bruise to disappear? One week? Two weeks? We were cruising the lesser streets on the Poniente side of town in Dad's car – a six-cylinder Ford Zodiac soft top that guzzled gas and belched fumes – in search of a particular restaurant that he knew was ready to close down. This restaurant was just one of the places Dad had his eye on at the time when his expansion ideas were starting to take shape. This venue was a sitting duck, he told me. The proprietors would soon be begging someone to take it off their hands. He himself had one hand on the steering wheel – his other hand trailed at the side of the car with the inevitable cigarette cupped inside it. We had to slow and then stop to allow a stray dog to make its lazy way across the road. It was as if Dad had come to a sudden and unexpected decision. He flicked his half-finished cigarette towards the dog, let go of the wheel, reached for the glove compartment, and brought out a packet of Rothmans. Then he opened the pack, shook out a filter-tipped cigarette, and held it up across the space between us.

'Do you use these things?' he asked without looking at me.

'No,' I said without thinking about it. It was a snap decision – right away, I understood it was the wrong thing to say. I could easily have taken a few puffs, couldn't I? I could have taken two or three harmless drags, but I elected not to. Or was I barking up the wrong tree completely? This whole cigarette business was a test – I didn't doubt that. But might it be a kind of double bluff? Was it better, or stronger, to reject the offer after all? It was another beautiful day.

The car was half in and half out of the sun, or the shade, depending on how you looked at it. It was obvious to me. My inability to call the Rothmans cigarette situation one way or the other was a mark of my emotional immaturity or inadequacy. It ought to have been easy. Instead, it was difficult. I was in a bind. I was damned if I did, and I was damned if I didn't. There was something wrong with me – there had to be. What was it? Was it a species of degeneracy, on a par with, say, masturbating daily? Abruptly, Dad pulled in at the side of the road and yanked the handbrake on, and in the moment of stillness that ensued I knew I faced some kind of reckoning.

'What do you think?' my father asked. 'Is it better to be on the sea front proper where the crowds are, or one block back from the beach where the rents and rates are lower?'

'I don't know,' I said. 'As you've more or less suggested, there are advantages to both propositions.'

'If a particular variety of pizza – chicken with pineapple, let's say – is your runaway top seller, is it sounder from a profit point of view to discount it or to up its unit price?'

'Again –' I said. 'I don't really know. An economist could give you an answer, but would it take sufficient account of the human factor? It isn't necessarily a black or white thing, is it? People don't always act the way you expect them to, it seems to me.'

'You're dead right about that, son. Take you, for instance –'

'What about me?' I said. All the signs were there, weren't they? The direction of travel was clear. If this was to be a conversation about Barbara, or about what we had done together in a crummy hotel bedroom, I was ready for it. 'What about me, Dad?'

'If you had to bribe someone – a petty official, let's imagine – to get a licence, say, or to carry a deal over the line, how would you feel about doing something like that?'

'I'd feel OK. I'd feel OK about it, I guess. Whatever it takes, right?'

'Ah, whatever it takes.' Here, my father lit a new cigarette from his old one and tossed the butt at a boarded-up Chinese restaurant across the street from where we were parked. 'There she blows,' he announced. 'Vacant possession. They went out of business because they couldn't, or wouldn't, stump up.'

'Stump up what?' I asked, even though I knew the answer. We were talking about some kind of bung or backhander, presumably. What was the point, though? Meaning what was the point right here and right now? I didn't have to wait long to find out.

'What do you want to do with your life, Keith?' There it was. Now we were getting somewhere – somewhere a bit closer to home. What was happening here? Was he picking a fight? Was my father picking a fight with me or not? I was on a vast prairie without any cover. There was a helicopter gunship in the sky up ahead. 'I don't suppose you can be a delivery boy forever –'

'I thought I might go to university,' I said as lightly as I could. Crazy, I know – in the current circumstances this simple statement had the force of a provocation. I had always dismissed the idea of university. Going to university would take money – Dad's money. There was only one place I wanted that money to go, and you know about that already. There we were in commercial Benidorm, one block back from the finest of beaches. It was a gorgeous day in high summer. I was sitting in my father's car. I was sitting in my father's old 2.6L Ford Zodiac convertible, waiting for him to hit me. What I mean is – I actually *wanted* him to hit me under the clear blue sky. Then he looked at me and I looked at him.

'What you did –' he said. 'Don't do it again, please. You know what I'm talking about, don't you?'

When I played this conversation back in the days to come it all made perfect sense. It made perfect sense to me in an unexpected way. My father had made himself clear on the question of his lover or his girlfriend. In fact, I had no plans to repeat or reprise the scene with Barbara. But there was something other than that. If my father was disappointed in me, the real cause, I suspected, lay elsewhere. What he wanted above all was for me to stand alongside him in the delivery of his business plan. When he asked me all those questions about bribes and best-selling pizzas he was giving me a sign – a sign of his approval. The fact that I had thought him a monster in that oh-so-masculine car of his struck me as shameful now. I wanted to make it up to him, but I didn't know how to do it. Then I changed my mind about the whole deal. I came to see the whole thing in a new light – a much less favourable light. My father was a bully. At all times he thought he knew exactly what was good for me. He was interested in my future only in so far as it aligned with his own vision or outlook. At a certain point I came to hate my father – something I had promised would never happen. I even began to cast around for ways of getting back at him. Didn't I tell you I was totally lost? That's how it was for me in the dog days of my Benidorm summer. I didn't know whether I was coming or going. Absolutely nothing was right. Everything was wrong under a cloudless sky.

Barbara returned, and life went on without major incident for a week or two. Then, on Saturday evening, I was summoned again to the Casa Hermosa on the edge of town. I was asked for by name by a charming woman who spoke perfect English, Barbara told me with a hint of pique in her voice. In other words, a certain parish of Javier's delivery landscape appeared to have been usurped by yours truly. (What I couldn't be expected to understand at this juncture was that my fellow courier's relationship with Fast Freddie's Diner was already history.) One thing was clear to me, and for this shred of reassurance I was most grateful. Whatever Barbara held against me – I couldn't be blamed for it. It wasn't my fault. I had no way of knowing for sure whether or not she had owned up to my father as part of a plea bargain arrangement at the centre of their recent reconciliation. I just presumed she *had*, and tried to put the whole business as far behind me as possible. In fact, distractions aplenty were coming at me on key fronts. OK – I lost my so-called cherry to Barbara. That much was technically true. There again, I'm not convinced it really counts unless various conditions are wholly met, or certain aspirations are adequately fulfilled. At the time I thought this only right and proper. I haven't changed my mind since.

It was as before. At the iron gates I removed my crash helmet and submitted my visage for inspection. In my arms were the three cardboard boxes – on each box the single word *funghi* was scrawled in Barbara's blue biro. Although the day was almost done it was too early for the aerobatic swooping of shrill birds. Instead, the noise of ten thousand cicadas flexing their tymbal membranes filled the hot, still air on either side of the driveway. Up ahead, the big blue sedan claimed a strip of deep shade alongside the great house, with doors, bonnet and boot flung wide open. This time, the Oldsmobile was attended by Paco – he was wiping the paintwork down powerfully with bucket and chamois leather in hand. When he stopped to look at me I had the sense he was sizing, or weighing, me up – it was as if he was trying to work out how easy it would be to knock me down. It unfolded just the way I had expected it to. The front door of the house yielded, as if in response to some agreed timetable, to reveal Isabella clothed from head to toe in white satin. I wasn't surprised to see her like that. In my overwrought imagination she was getting ready to submerge herself in a bath of unicorn's milk. Nothing she said or did was capable of surprising me – to that extent I had long ago fallen under her spell.

'You rang, mademoiselle?' I said from the steps of the porch. 'Three mushroom pizzas to take away – or to *go*, as our American friends might say. To go is certainly expressive, but will it catch on?'

Again, she invited me to wait while she withdrew to check the order. In point of fact, she told me her uncle would check the order. That was his role in all this. Now I got it. Now I understood where the third pizza fitted in. The sister and brother lived here with their uncle, their guardian. His was an influential but veiled presence, I decided. He was rarely seen around the house or city. I heard the barking from behind me of the dogs. Then Paco appeared as if from nowhere with two slavering hounds on short leads before vanishing into the low sun. She was back. She told me she had something that belonged to me. She led me down a corridor hung with paintings in heavy frames towards a shuttered room lined with bookcases and dominated by a four-poster bed. She made me wait beside the bed while she disappeared into an adjoining chamber. Was it his room? Was it Manolito's room? All around and glimpsed by candlelight were the books in many languages. There was a picture of a ruined lighthouse, figment of a dream, on the wall above the fireplace, and – incongruously, somehow, to my mind – a graduation photograph of Isabella wearing mortar board and gown taken on a dull day in Oxford or similar. When she returned she gave me back my wallet, but not before kissing it theatrically and opening it up to reveal its contents, still visibly intact, like a fortune teller in a travelling show. 'Abracadabra,' she whispered, pressing a finger against my lips as if to silence me for my own good, or in my own best interests.

Isabella's proposition was simple. In return for my stolen wallet I would make love to her now on the four-poster bed. After she let her silky kimono fall to the floor she stood naked in front of me for a moment in order to let me admire her body. Then she undressed me slowly – all this time I was wondering what to do with the insect-spattered helmet I had been carrying under one arm. In the end it was Manolito who relieved me of this comical burden. That's right – the sister and the brother were both with me now on the groaning bed. I recall thinking I was probably in need of a shower and a bar of soap. Meanwhile, a characteristic floral fragrance lent the heavy air a top note of innocence. For the record – we did nothing to write home about on that bed as a multitude of candles hissed all around us. Was it perverse, or perverted? Was it wrong? I mean the brother and sister double act? To me, it was funny. I laughed, and soon the two siblings laughed, and with that their spell was broken. At least, that's what I wanted to believe as I descended their drive with the greedy birdsong in the sky above me. How could I have known they weren't quite finished with their English friend yet?

There was an unlikely postscript to this bizarre encounter with the Casa Hermosa and its denizens – a twist in the unexpected tale. Javier was waiting for me on his motorbike at the third bend in the road that led from the gated finca towards the downtown zone. He warned me in Spanish to be careful. Those people are bad, he said in English. Those people are *perros periculosos*. When I invited him to explain himself he gunned his engine twice. 'Do you enjoy to make naked swimming?' he asked boldly – no, shyly – as if he had scoured his pocket Spanish-English dictionary in search of an eternal verity, stammering gamely all the while. What could I do? I said yes.

THE FOLLOWING DAY – A SUNDAY – WAS A SAINT'S DAY or a feast day or something like that. Dad closed the restaurant directly after lunchtime service as planned, and we all took the rest of the day off.

I met Javier as arranged on the promenade behind a busy *playa poniente*. He pumped my hand somewhat stiffly, or awkwardly, and I took a picture of him scowling from the rail and backlit by the sun with his rolled-up towel tucked under one arm and his crash helmet wedged below the other. He told me straight away he was no longer working as a delivery boy at my father's diner. When I asked him why that was, he first spat at the sand and then kissed me hard on the mouth. On the beach in front of us, a series of Super-8 movies played out colourfully in an endless loop. The throbbing sky – was it aquamarine or ultramarine? I didn't know – I only knew blue was too small a word for it.

We found a spot close to the shoreline and claimed it using two helmets placed suitably apart on the hot sand. Next, we had to get changed – this meant worming out of and into key items with towels wrapped around us. Javier's swimming costume turned out to be a pair of cut-off jeans very similar to what he had just removed. Mine was the normal skimpy affair most unsuited to hiding or disguising the least sign of arousal. I tried not to think about that – it wouldn't have been helpful. When I made to take another picture of Javier with the silver sea behind him he told me it was unmanly. It looked unmanly, he said, to anyone who was watching. He was probably right about that. For a while he sat beside me on his towel, running the fine sand through his fingers, and I had a ludicrous urge, which I resisted bravely, to have him bury me up to my neck in the stuff. That would definitely have looked unmanly to anyone watching us. Javier began to tell me about the islet in the bay, but I wasn't really listening to him. The island was the site of a peacock farm – I only apprehended this peculiar detail after my companion pretended to be an ungainly bird with a large, decorative tail. If I wasn't paying a great deal of attention to what he was saying it was only because

I was increasingly aware of how he was saying it. It was true. I said nothing at the time, but it was nonetheless true – Javier no longer stammered like it was going out of fashion, and this made me wildly happy on his behalf. When a rubber ball from a nearby game struck him on the chest he threw it high into the air above us. It was a kind of marker for something, I realised – a turning point for my friend in the context of this day of all days, or, rather, of what he wanted from this scenario and from me. 'Now we make naked swimming,' he announced gravely, and charged towards the shallows.

The sea, which was dead calm, got deeper only very gradually. We waded out until it was up to our shoulders. Then Javier took me onto his back and gave me a turtle ride. He took it for granted that he was a better swimmer than I was – he was right. We were a good distance from the shoreline when he shrugged me off and turned to face me. After he removed his shorts he laid them on the surface of the water – this for the avoidance of any doubt, I decided. Quickly, I did the same with my own swimming costume. Soon we got down to business. I did it for him, and then he did it for me – or he tried to. In my case, something got in the way. I kept imagining we were about to be interrupted from below by a passing jellyfish or a nosy shark. Once this impression took hold it was difficult to shake it off. We swam hastily back towards the shore, but not before Javier was obliged to dive deep underwater in order to retrieve my trunks, by then roughly half way to the bottom of the Mediterranean Sea. My friend was an exceptional swimmer – looking back, I think this was one of the factors that tipped the balance for me. Funny how these things work, or don't work, out. At all events, you have to go along with them, ready or not.

The sting had begun to go out of the afternoon sun when Javier revealed he had a surprise for me. In the shadow of an unmanned lifeguard's chair not far from our spot on the beach he unearthed a large plastic bottle filled with a local red wine. The bottle was still cool – after we rinsed off the sand we settled down under the high chair and passed the booty back and forth between us. I had never drunk red wine before. Perhaps I shouldn't have drunk any then. It was still hot, and our inadequate supply of drinking water had long ago run out. I asked Javier about his family. Then I wished I hadn't. It was all too clear he didn't want to talk about his home life, and I had no intention of pressing him on the subject. He was just like I was in many respects. Although my first instinct was to see him as something dangerous or exotic – a peacock, for example, or a shark – I quickly came to regret this point of view, which was unworthy of both Javier and me. All the while it was waiting to ambush us – this whole matter of why my friend no longer worked at my father's diner. It turned out Javier had been dismissed, sacked, for stealing from the till. He blurted this out unbidden and uninvited when our bottle of wine was about three-quarters empty. Barbara, it was, who did the dirty work. Poor Javier – he was at pains now not to criticise or disparage Dad in any way to my face. 'I never steal this money,' he protested with big, angry tears in his eyes. 'Never, never. For sure my father beat me good when he find out –'

What happened after that is not completely clear to me. I had to piece a lot of it together from what Barbara told me later. When I got back to Fast Freddie's at about seven o'clock she was with Dad at a small table eating supper and drinking wine.

'You shouldn't have sacked Javier for stealing from the till,' I told her straight off.

'Oh?' she said, getting up fast from the table. They were both on their feet now with their fancy napkins in their hands. 'Are you all right? You look a little the worse for wear.'

'Are you drunk, Keith?' my father asked with a hint of amused disbelief in his voice.

'You shouldn't have dismissed Javier for stealing from the till, Barbara,' I insisted.

'Oh?' she said again. 'And why is that, tell me?'

'Because it was me who stole from the till.' Here, I parked my camera very carefully on the nearest table out of harm's way. Then I drew out my Swiss army knife and opened it up lovingly. 'Do you recognise this clever little number, Dad? You gave it to me for my thirteenth birthday. You said I was ready for it. I always thought it would come in handy for *something*. It has a toothpick and tweezers and a tiny pair of scissors you can use for lots of different activities.'

'Give that to me, please,' my father said. 'Give it to me – before you hurt someone.'

'You'll have to take it off me,' I told him, backing away as he dropped his napkin to the floor.

'Give it to me, Keith,' he repeated, waving Barbara aside and starting towards me.

After I discarded my beloved Swiss army knife I rushed at my father and allowed various blows to rain down on him for a short while. In fact, he allowed various blows to rain down on him. Then he wrestled me to the floor and sat on my chest, and I begged him over and over again to hit me until he shut me up finally by slapping me hard across the face. He slapped me twice, Barbara reported. I don't understand why I stole from the till. No doubt a novice shrink would make short work of the thing. I gave the cash back right away – of course, I did. It was never really about the funds, was it? Dad's money – I *never* wanted any for myself. After he helped me up from the floor that night he took me in his arms and told me everything was going to be fine. If only I could have believed him. I had a long, cold shower up in my room, and then I changed into my Benidorm best – khaki trousers and a pale blue linen bush shirt I had ironed myself – because the most important part of the evening was still to come. On the table beside my bed sat my bulging wallet, retrieved recently from the Casa Hermosa, and glaring at me like a warning. I could barely bring myself to look at it. I couldn't bear to think of the role it might yet play in my disastrous life.

It was dark and cool. The long day was almost done. As I stood by my sad phone box, waiting for my mother to lift the receiver at her end, I counted out the number of rings before she answered. It was a harmless little game I played with myself. Actually, it was far from harmless. To me, it was a matter of life and death. Twenty-six rings tonight – a new world record. I had been about to give up, to go back to my room. I was all set to hang up after thirty rings. When she answered finally it was the same as always. She was completely drunk, and scarcely able to speak. She repeated my name with long pauses in between. After a minute or so I told her I loved her. I told her I would call her at the same time next Sunday. I waited for her to say goodbye, but she never did. After I hung up it took me a long time to let go of the phone. I didn't want to let go of it.

PART THIRD

Legacies of Love

I FELL IN LOVE WITH JAVIER QUICKLY. How long does it generally take? In my case it took about ten days or a fortnight. I tried not to – I swear I did. It was the very definition of unmanly, was it not? I tried, but it was useless – his natural combination of toughness and vulnerability proved irresistible over the course of those few fateful weeks. At first, I wanted to be like him. Soon I actually wanted to *be* him in a way that struck me as alarming and dizzying both. I was doomed from the beginning.

All this time I was kept even busier than usual at Fast Freddie's Diner. My father was recruiting for a second restaurant he planned to open soon. This one, a pizza parlour first and foremost, was on the other side of town – Dad said the district was on the up and up. Barbara offered Javier his old job at the new place, but he turned her down. He had landed an apprenticeship with the postal service, he told me proudly. He was still a delivery boy at heart, he said, but now he had a career. Meanwhile, a new delivery *man* was set to join us at Fast Freddie's Diner. You couldn't really call him a boy – his hair was already greying. As I say – I was kept very busy while this new delivery person got to know the ropes. I went to bed dog tired each night after stealing a few kisses from Javier at suitable locations around the city. Kisses and fumblings were one thing – in my heart

I knew that something more would have to come after. Already, my friend was investigating set-ups for rendezvous, liaisons and trysts – options distanced physically and psychologically from his home. It was clear to me where we were going with this. When Javier asked me if I was still doing the famous Casa Hermosa pizza delivery run every second Saturday night, I told him I was. When I asked him again what he had meant when he said I should be careful in those parts, he failed to enlarge. He said it again – these were bad people – and left it at that. I had the idea he was holding out on me, but there was little I could do about it. I had long had the feeling my friend was equipped with a strong sense of justice and fairness. Was he shielding me from an unwholesome truth? Perhaps it was better for me not to know. It was a local matter. It was the kind of thing I had no business with. I didn't have to wait much longer to get to the bottom of it. Do you recall Mr Salvadori, the lonely man given to maladroit public statements of the bodily sort? He was about to come into, or back into, my life in an unforgettable way.

It was raining. That is the first thing to say, or to record. I don't think it had rained once during my Benidorm summer to date – at least not by day. The rain set in at lunchtime, scattering the diners at the pavement tables along the strip, and continued all afternoon and evening. It was a novel feature, an event. The kids loved it. The mongrel dogs disdained it, sulking under the same parked vans and trucks they usually favoured for their shade. For me on my delivery rounds the rain had nuisance value only. It had little practical effect other than to slow me down and get me wet. Or so I thought.

When I stepped out of the lift on the tenth floor, Mr Salvadori was waiting for me as normal a short distance away in the doorway of his flat. There was something different, however, on this occasion – of his clumsy social engagement tactic there was no sign. It was a surprise – an alert freighted with implication. Change, or risk, was in the air – I felt this keenly in an obscure way. First, there was the rain to consider, and now Mr Salvadori. As I prised his pizza from the top of the stash inside my shoulder bag, I paused to confirm the designation written on the box in Barbara's hand. What I saw there was not what I expected to see. What it should have said on the box was *pepperoni*, in line with Mr Salvadori's liking for sausage. Instead, it said *funghi*, or mushroom. On the other hand, the box was placed uppermost on the pile – first, in other words, for delivery. Naturally, I rooted around in my insulated sack seeking answers. It was a little uncanny. All four boxes bore the popular *funghi* label of the hour. Something was wrong – I sensed this intuitively, but I didn't act on my gut feeling. I should have checked with Mr Salvadori there and then. That was my mistake. OK – it was only the latest in a series of blunders spanning a broad range of histories. Let's just say I was distracted by rogue weather at a key moment. Call it a lame excuse if you will – I won't try to stop you. Fate set the trap, and I walked right into it, damp cardboard boxes in hand.

By the time I approached the floodlit villa with my remaining three pizza boxes in tow, the rain had all but stopped and the first stars were visible in the clearing sky. Much more significant – I was in a panic. I couldn't shake off the idea that I had given the wrong pizza to Mr Salvadori as part of a simple mix-up, an administrative error. At a certain level it was no more complicated than that. Even so, something told me there was danger up ahead. It had to do with the Casa Hermosa and all who sailed in her. Again, I heard Javier's warning. These were bad people – wasn't that his message? To say I had a negative feeling about everything under the moon and the stars at this time would be to do my anxiety levels a disservice. I felt very alone – that was the abiding sense I had.

Just short of the familiar iron gates I pointed my scooter at the perimeter wall so that the headlight shone back at me weakly. As I considered my three pizza boxes in turn I became more and more convinced of it – inside one of these innocent repositories lurked Mr Salvadori's spicy sausage order. What happened next was shocking to me. When I opened the first cardboard box I discovered several tightly packed decks of used banknotes in denominations of 5,000 pesetas. Immediately, I closed the box and returned it to my sack. Then I took it out again and, with unsteady hand, counted the cash as best I could. I counted about one hundred banknotes in that first box. What did it mean? It meant the hoard was worth over £2,500 according to my rough calculations. Inside the second box I found a further £500 worth of banknotes, this time in denominations of 1,000 Pts. When I opened the third box I nearly cried out. There it was for anyone to see – Mr Salvadori's preferred pizza, its signature slices gleaming silkily in the interested starlight.

Yes, it was a shock. My mouth was bone dry. I felt sick. All the same, I understood very well what was happening here. It was clear to me from the off – the money I was sitting on represented some sort of insurance or protection payment made on a regular basis by the proprietors of Fast Freddie's Diner to the occupants of the Casa Hermosa. I got it, but I didn't know what to do about it. Something was knocking loudly on the door of my troubled consciousness. It was all about the fourth, which is really to say the first, pizza box – the one I had parted company with half an hour ago on the tenth floor of a high-rise block in downtown Benidorm. What was in that box? That was the sixty-four-thousand-dollar question in my book. Was it a mushroom pizza, or something quite different – something much more valuable, for example? In the end, the pressing need to decide what to do next was taken out of my sticky hands. Suddenly and silently, the big gates swept open beside me and a disembodied voice split the night. 'Come in, Keith –' Manolito said. 'We've been expecting you.'

I had to go through with it. Manolito accepted the three boxes from me in a brightly lit porch and took them away for his uncle to check. When he came back he told me the order was wrong. I could have told him that, but I gave nothing away to Manolito – he of the cruel mouth and the predatory instinct.

'Go back, please, Keith,' he commanded smoothly, 'and pick up the correct order. We always have a third mushroom pizza – I thought you knew that by now.'

'Let me see what I can do,' I said. 'They don't often make such a basic error in our kitchen.'

There was a grim inevitability about what happened after that. If you make a mistake, you own the consequences. In my defence I can only say I wasn't exclusively to blame. At heart, it was an issue of slack communications, of faulty process. One of my stout boxes was wrongly labelled. That was it in a nutshell. Chance set the trap, and I jumped in with both feet.

As I stood outside Mr Salvadori's apartment, my finger on the bell, I began to doubt my powers of reason. At one point I actually thought I must be on the wrong floor of the building. The lights of the landing were on a timer – every so often they cut out, plunging the corridor into darkness. There came no sound from behind Mr Salvadori's door – not a peep. Then it occurred to me with a slightly chilling effect – the little name plate once located below the spy hole had been removed from the front door of the flat. Mr Salvadori had gone away, it seemed, at short notice.

When I got back to Fast Freddie's I demanded to see Dad right way. It was unfortunate, Barbara said – he had been detained at a posh dinner organised annually by the local business community in honour of itself. I really wanted to tell Barbara what had happened. Wasn't she practically the joint master, or mistress, of the house? What was it she told me on my very first day in Benidorm? It was dog eat dog in this dirty town, she said. For some reason I couldn't bring myself to discuss what I knew with Barbara. I was custodian of a dangerous secret. The less anyone knew about it the better.

I hardly slept that night. I was thinking about Javier, and about how much I missed him. I thought about my mother, too. Was she asleep on the sofa now, surrounded by her empty bottles? All this is to say I was doing my miserable best to take my mind off the night's drama, and my eye off the locked door to my room. At any moment I expected someone uncouth to shoot the lock off in a bid to recover absent funds. I had no idea what I would do in those circumstances. At some point I must have dozed off. There are times when you go to sleep and you really don't want to wake up. Soon I was dreaming of Mr Salvadori. He was taking a short holiday, or a sabbatical, in order to put recent events behind him. He was living it up on a jet plane bound for Paris or London or Rome. No – he had his sights set on Acapulco or Rio. There were distractions here aplenty for a shy and retiring man like Mr Salvadori. As for his personal loyalty to me – I guess it didn't stretch as far as I thought it did.

THE DAY OF TRUTH DAWNED NOT SO MUCH visibly as audibly for me. There was a persistent ringing sound, difficult to explain and harder to ignore, inside my head. The characteristic sensation I had was of confusion, resignation and denial. I was fully prepared to roll over for an extra hour, this being Sunday. At the same time I had a nagging feeling, urgent and growing more so with each ring, that today was a big day for me. Then it came to me – the telephone in my room, which I had managed effortlessly to overlook for weeks, was doing what it was designed to do. It was ringing.

Five minutes later I presented myself two floors below in line with my father's injunction. I had my trusty wallet in my hip pocket, where it very naturally belonged. What role was it destined to play today? Was it a form of insurance? Insurance against what, exactly? I had no firm or fixed idea. I was caught up in a kind of protection racket of the body and soul, with my next payment due at any time. There was otherwise little to see here. Only my lifelong happiness was at stake. The clock said ten. All Benidorm was at breakfast. The eggs were flying, sunny side up for preference, off the griddle at Fast Freddie's Diner, a popular local eatery. Not for the first time in this dog-eat-dog town, my heart was in my mouth.

The conversation, which I had expected to focus early on the mushroom-pizza-slash-missing-funds imbroglio of the night before, took a different turn from the start. Doubtless several subjects were up for grabs here. Juicy talking points fairly queued up for debate when it came to my conduct that summer in Spain. My father had very recently had a letter from my mother – this in response to his own missive of a month ago. Now I saw how, or where, my bulging wallet fitted into today's story.

'Your mother,' my father began, 'never received that money.'

'Oh?' I said, not exactly playing for time. I didn't need to play for time. Why would I? I had nothing left to lose. I had nothing left to lose except the tiniest shred of dignity I kept in reserve for special occasions – occasions not unlike this one, in fact. 'What money was that?' I asked now. 'Perhaps you can refresh my memory, Dad –'

'The money you left in an envelope before you flew to Spain.'

'Of course – *that* money. I might have known it would rear its head again. The most likely reason why Mum never got the money is because it's actually here in my pocket.' I was a magician pulling rabbits from a hat. It was perfect. My wallet, which was once lost, was now found. After I spread its contents, taking in cash, travellers' cheques, sketch map and directions for travel, on a vacant table my father looked at me for a moment without speaking. Poor Dad – I guess he just picked the wrong guy. I guess he just chose the wrong son. 'It's all there,' I told him. 'Why don't you count it? It's all there, apart from the money I spent on a taxi to the airport in London. In fact, you've made a profit on the transaction because someone – a Good Samaritan, if you like – gave me a lift from Alicante airport all the way to sunny Benidorm.'

'Why did you lie, Keith? Why did you lie about the money?'

It was a good question. What could I possibly say now to make it easier on my father? After I lost my wallet I didn't want to appear weak in front of him – you know about that already. The point is – I really had wanted the money to go to my mother. I couldn't worry about the drinking. When I said I'd given away the cash it was an act of wish fulfilment, slightly desperate, but nonetheless sincere.

'It was a kind of white lie,' I told my father sadly in answer to his question. 'You won't believe me when I tell you what happened, but I'm going to tell you anyway.'

Then I gave him the story in its purest form. I lost my wallet, and then I found it again somewhere down the line. I said nothing of Isabella and Manolito. What good would that have done? All the time I was talking my father eyed me keenly, as if he was observing a talented circus animal, or an exotic species in the wild. 'The truth is I didn't want to look weak in front of you,' I told him finally. 'Is that so terrible, Dad? Is that so wrong?'

First, he nodded at me for what seemed like a long time. Then he took up my wallet, replaced the various contents I had scattered on the table, and gave the whole lot back to me. The matter – this matter – was evidently closed. Now, presumably, was an ideal time to discuss mushroom pizzas, which were a runaway bestseller this season. People couldn't get enough of them.

'I think it's probably time for you to go back to Scotland,' my father said. 'It'll take me a few days to make the arrangements, of course. I don't think you're cut out for this, Keith.'

'This what?' I asked my father hotly because I was hurt.

'What happened last night –' he said without answering me directly. 'I've already taken care of it for you. I presume it was an innocent mistake. At any rate, your friends on the edge of town are very grateful for a successful outcome. They want to make it up to you somehow – I mean for any bad feeling.'

It sounded to me like a threat, and that's exactly what it proved to be. I have to believe my father knew nothing of their ugly intent – that would be too much to bear. I didn't really care about what they gave me that night – not as such. It was the collateral damage, as in the knock-on effect over time, that really did for me.

At about eight o'clock I was lying in Javier's arms on my little bed two floors above my father's restaurant. I no longer worked at Fast Freddie's Diner. Neither my friend nor I worked there now. If I couldn't quite bring myself to tell Javier I would soon be leaving town, it wasn't because I thought the news would upset him unduly. In fact, I imagined he would get over it – and me – in a few short days. No – it was for my own sake that I said nothing. The idea of exchanging this home for that one filled me with dread. I distrusted the future. Its undisclosed ambition was to *find me out*. Meanwhile, it was still Sunday. It was Sunday all day. That's right – it was time for me to leave a lover's embrace and make my weekly pilgrimage to the phone station on the promenade beside the sheltering sea. I couldn't bring myself to make the journey. I even considered using the telephone in my room to make long-distance contact at this, the eleventh, hour. If only I had known what to do with the apparatus. Then it kicked off – the last meaningful act of my ill-fated summer. First, the handle of my locked door flexed and settled. Then came the knocking, soft but insistent.

'Keith? It's Manolito. Please open the door. There's something I want to give you.'

Javier jumped up and started pulling on his clothes. I did the same things. When I opened the door, Manolito stepped forward to occupy the threshold of the room. He looked different. Usually, he wore something loose and floppy – an embroidered smock, say, or a kaftan. Today, or tonight, he had on a black suit, very tight, with a white shirt and a red tie. His hair, slicked back brilliantly, looked darker than I recalled. When he spoke, his voice sounded changed – it was deeper, perhaps, or coarser.

'Ah, yes – Javier is there too. That's nice. How sweet. I'm sure we all know why we're here. We're here for you, my English friend. You are our principal focus tonight. We have loved you in our way, Keith. That is why I hope you'll come to view this as a token of our undying regard –'

They were amoralists. They recognised no rules-based system of behaviour. They had got what they wanted, but it wasn't enough. It would never be sufficient. After he clicked his fingers, Manolito backed away to permit Paco ingress. Javier pushed himself in front of me, but I thrust him roughly aside. No one was going to steal my thunder on this gala occasion. The quiet henchman, dressed all in trademark white, aimed his gun at my foot and fired two rounds in quick succession, after which the visitors left the stage. It occurred to me again – there was pathos and there was bathos in the life of a delivery boy. Then I remembered I was no longer a delivery boy, and fainted clean away. I never got to make my scheduled call that Sunday night after all. Instead, I attended an emergency healthcare facility this side of midnight. My phone call didn't take place, which was a tragic turn of events. You might say I broke a sacred promise, or an immutable campaign pledge. It was my last major mistake of the summer holiday, and I've paid for it in bitter tears ever since.

MY MOTHER CHOKED ON HER own vomit. That was the cause of death on the certificate. In truth, of course, the actual cause of her death was her *life*, lived as it was latterly in a spirit and attitude of wilful destructiveness and neglect. I don't believe, and neither did the coroner, she intended to bring the curtain down in such a finite way. She gave no indication of that. Doubtless she continues to float in a sunlit realm high above the clouds, counting her empty bottles and waiting for the telephone to ring. It was a concerned neighbour with a spare key who discovered her. I was grateful for that. It meant I didn't have to discover her myself.

Barbara and I left Benidorm on a ravishing morning in a taxi paid for in advance by my father. He was a very busy man in those days. His second restaurant had just opened triumphantly, and he had plans for a third. I had expected him to convey me personally to Alicante airport as a way of locating my departure beyond the range of further misfortune. In the event, Barbara acted as mission guarantor and chaperone for the whole of my journey. And she got it. She got *me*. In the matter of my impaired mobility, for example, she was particularly thoughtful from the start. When I asked if our driver might make a small detour in order to take in Javier's house she understood immediately what was happening. She even had to identify the right address for me, which struck me as unaccountably poignant. By this generous action, it seemed to me, we were bound together irrevocably. We were sitting side by side in the back of the taxi with my crutches propped over the front seat beside the long-suffering driver. I said goodbye to my best friend through the open window of the car. My sudden leaving was a shock to poor Javier – I could see that. I didn't mention my mother's death. I don't think I had actually spoken of her to Javier all summer. Stammering very slightly in the way I thought he'd got over, he said he would write to me in imperfect English if I could give him an address. Absurd, I know – I had already written the address on the front of an airmail envelope in case he should ask. Whether it would still be my address tomorrow, or the day after, was unclear. I didn't say anything about that to Javier. Then we shook hands awkwardly and I told the taxi driver to go. I waved at my friend through the window as we pulled away from the kerb. I never expected to see him, nor to hear from him, again. Pretty soon it came to me – there was a latent image of Javier sitting inside my Pentax camera, waiting to be developed. As I left Benidorm and its dazzling beaches behind me, the idea or the fact of this image meant a lot to me. At some point Barbara asked me if I was all right. Like I say – she got it. I was thinking about my mother as the Spanish scenery, so vivid and brutal, rolled past us. At a certain moment in time my mother had sought oblivion, and now she had, to all intents and purposes, found it. As our car pulled up at the terminal building, I felt sure she was happier now. And in a cruel twist of fate, I too had got what I wanted. I had often enough wished my mother dead – and now she was.

For the flight to London there were certain logistical protocols which had to do with my bandaged foot and my crutches and how to get me to the plane in the best way. Barbara handled everything superbly. She had a window seat above the wing of the 737, and I

123

sat beside the aisle not far away with my leg protruding necessarily from time to time. Although we didn't say very much we were close, Barbara and I, on that sad journey. I felt this without trying. Our experience of the Spanish coast had allied us in an indefinable but undeniable way. I think Barbara felt this too. What else to say about our passage to England? Funny thing – I had no use for the sick bag from this end to that.

The funeral took place on a warm, rather humid morning at a crematorium on the outskirts of Glasgow. Mourners were thin on the ground that day. As I sat with Barbara in the frontmost pew of the chapel I sensed a great weight or presence behind me. When I turned to look, no one else was there. We had lunch – just the two of us – at the Arnott Simpson department store in the city centre, but not before the last act played out in a garden of remembrance in the grounds of the crematorium. In the end, of course, it proved to be something other than the final chapter, but that is a different story. As we cast around for a suitable place to scatter my mother's ashes, me hobbling on my crutches all the while, Barbara lobbed a conversational grenade into the muggy air.

'I'm not going back, Keith,' she announced quietly. 'I thought you would want to know.'

'What are you talking about?' I asked, although I understood exactly what she was telling me and how significant it was.

'I'm not going back to Benidorm,' she said. 'I'm going home to Macclesfield instead. That's where my roots are. That's where I belong – where it rains from one Sunday to the next and the nearest beach is confined to a lively corner of the imagination.'

'Oh,' I said. 'And what will you do there, I wonder?'

'Open a coffee shop,' she said. 'If it does well, I'll open a second one. You can come and work for me next summer, if you like.'

'Well, I never —' I said. 'That's a turn up for the books.' It was. It really was. As I sat down on a bench to rest my leg and to process these developments, I lost sight of Barbara for a moment. She was telling me something in her courteous and thoughtful way. She was sharing something important about my father — that's what she was doing in a manicured garden under a leaden sky. She probably saw it as a necessary part of my sentimental education, to which she had already contributed a great deal.

'What about here?' she called out purposefully from over my right shoulder 'There's a lovely perfume coming from these mature rose bushes. Do you think she'd like that?'

'Oh, yes,' I said. 'She always liked flowers.' Suddenly, it came to me — what I really wanted to do with my mother's ashes. It would take time to organise, of course. These things usually did. It might take half a lifetime, plus or minus, to get the job done. So what if it did? In the end it would be worth it. 'Hold your horses, over there,' I called out to Barbara. 'I've just had an idea.'

THE PRETTY RESORT TOWN OF PUERTO POLLENSA sits in a broad bay at the northern tip of Majorca, close to the rugged Formentor promontory. We took the precipitous road which rises, twisting and turning, from the fertile plain behind the capital and which follows the island's west coast as far as Pollensa itself — the main settlement is set back from the sea to guard against sudden pirate attack. Here, we fully expected to conclude our business before checking into the pre-booked Hotel Mirador, a three-star affair with private balconies looking out across the water. Our scripted arrangements, however, were blown off course at an early stage.

It was a Sunday — that was the principal obstacle in our path. The more Javier remonstrated with an out-of-hours representative of our preferred funeral parlour, the deeper the chap dug his heels in. If the visiting party could only wait until Monday or Tuesday, everything would be fine. A licence had already been issued in line with Spanish legal requirements. Seaworthy vessels of all sizes and specifications came and went freely from the southern wall of the marina. These boats sailed at the drop of a hat – but not, alas, on Sunday. Javier was for rescheduling the event, but I was adamant.

'It has to be a Sunday,' I told my exasperated friend, who also happened to be my constant companion. 'Don't ask me why.'

'But *why* does it have to be a Sunday?' he persisted in English, shaking his head.

'It just does,' I said tiredly. 'We can wait a week, or a fortnight, or we can go ahead with it tonight. I don't mind – but it has to be a Sunday. I'm sorry –'

'Tonight?' Javier said, rolling his eyeballs. 'As in *this very night*? Are you telling me you have a plan B up your sleeve?'

You can call it plan B if that satisfies you. To my mind, it was inevitable all along – I mean from the dawn of time. It was what I wanted. It was how I had pictured it since the idea first came to me in a garden of remembrance in Glasgow's east end. It was all about the ashes – ashes past, ashes present. My father's remains were in an urn in a niche set into a wall in the cemetery at Torrevieja on the mainland. Or, at least, they used to be. Who knows what happens when your original option lapses, and you fail to extend a ten-year lease? Sorry, Dad – I mean for everything. Time passes, and things look different. If you're lucky, you might even come to forget. And now it was time to let go of my mother at long last.

We set out at dusk from our hotel on the front – this after we had bought candles and jam jars from an open-minded chandler opposite the marina. It was October, but the sea was still warm. In practice, of course, the water is often at its warmest quite late in the year when the sun has been on it for a full summer. Javier pushed my wheelchair into the shallows and kept pushing until I told him to stop. Now the water was up to my chest. This was at the section of the beach which was located furthest from the boats and which faced directly south across the big bay. Once again, the sea was flat calm. It was always flat calm in my imagination, just as it had been on the day I first swam with Javier many years ago. Again, he took me on his back, then struck out for a horizon dark now and getting darker with each stroke. After a few minutes we stopped by mutual agreement, and I opened the small casket and sprinkled the meagre ashes on the sea with my back to the brooding land. It was all over very quickly. Suddenly, I felt cold.

'*Muchas gracias, querido,*' I said to Javier. 'I can die happy now.'

'*No hay de qué,*' he said. 'But please don't croak until we get back to the beach at the very least.'

'That's nice,' I said, shivering a little now. 'Do you remember what we did, or *made,* that afternoon in Benidorm?'

'Naked swimming, you mean?' he said. 'How could I forget? Ha! You chickened out at the last minute.'

'I don't remember that,' I said. 'I do recall falling in love with you that day, though, under a hopelessly blue sky.'

'What? Just one day it took you?' he said. 'You must have been desperate, *hombre* – that's all I can say.'

'Shall we go back now?' I asked. 'I don't think we should stay out here for too long. Isn't this when the big fish like to feed?'

'Don't be afraid,' he said. 'I'll catch you if you fall. Come on – climb aboard. I can't see the land, but I can smell the trees –'

As we swam towards an invisible shoreline it seemed the whole world had been struck dumb – no, struck dead. It was so dark. Were we too low down? Yes, that was it – the earth rose and then dipped ahead of us, and we were too low down here to see the lights of the town strung out somewhere to our left. Had we fallen from the sky and drowned? Who would mourn us in that case? For a moment we didn't exist, and I felt a profound sense of peace. Then we saw what we were looking for. She was guiding us in loyally from the edge of the water. Barbara was waiting for us there, ever faithful, with two candles raised in jam jars above her head. When it was all over, she helped Javier haul my wheelchair in, wading strongly out to sea in Jesus sandals and leotard. She didn't ask whether or not our mission had been successful. What could possibly go wrong out there where dark sky met darker sea? Barbara had this whole thing covered. She got it. She was all right by me.

We three said goodbye to Pollensa early the next morning. It was the launch of their big festival – the citizens were preparing to repel costumed corsairs from the streets of the town. A part of my mother resides there now in a place she always loved but never got to enjoy when the sun was at its highest point. I, for one, would like to go back there. It's a charming location – I can tell you that right now. At all times it has a great deal to offer the discerning visitor.

Under the Bridge at Midnight

ACT ONE

The Arrest

THEY CAME FOR ME AT MIDNIGHT – ON THE CUSP, in other words, of tomorrow. Was it the end or the beginning? It could have swung either way. It was a fifty-fifty situation. The clamour of their convoy hailed from nowhere – that is, from no obvious direction – growing in volume and intensity as the paddy-wagons rumbled from street to shuttered street of our cowed and curfewed city. This used to be London. I mean it used to be *called* London. At first I imagined the malevolent sirens were directed at somewhere else, at some*one* else – someone other than me. Or was this, once again, those masked and hooded refuse junkies arrived from beyond the city limits in a fleet of souped-up ambulances to raid with tacit official licence and more or less at random our metropolitan garbage cans heavy with microprocessors and semiconductors? Then it struck me obligingly – it was happening exactly the way Samuelson had proposed earlier when he took in my cat. The clamour – it was for my sake only.

At this time I was busy shredding the last of my written records and historical documents pertaining to the war – the war of famine and drought, the war to end all wars, or, more correctly, the war to end society. Much of this raw material had already been committed bravely to memory by youthful members of our group at home and abroad in a meticulous and arduous fashion frankly reminiscent of

131

the old science fiction novels. If only we had such stories today, our young people lament at dawn after another lonely night of learning by rote. The younger these minds are the better – that way the seed of truth lands on softer, more fertile ground where it takes root after a short struggle and sometime later blossoms in the dark. Who said the oral tradition was dead?

Now the air fell silent. The police convoy, which comprised, I quickly discovered, no less than five human transportation vehicles, drew up outside, as in directly below, my apartment. There came a violent banging on the front door at street level accompanied by uncouth shouts and cries. Almost at the same time, the front door was aggressively breached from without, and less than ten seconds later they were, six of them, inside my bachelor's flat on the second floor. The upper door they had no occasion to assault – I had left it unlocked and ajar just half a minute earlier.

For a startled (on their side) moment, there was utter silence. I counted four semi-automatic weapons, including what I took to be an old Luger, plus an angry-looking crowbar, about the uniformed persons of my uninvited but in no sense unexpected guests. Then one of them, their pistol-toting champion, stepped forward in a sea of shredded papers and lowered the scarlet bandana from around his nose and mouth. 'I hereby place you under arrest,' he declared redundantly but with an obscure emotion, as if to say *no, no – this one hundredth nocturnal intervention I view as lovingly as the first.*

'Arrest?' I countered with an air of calm, revisiting gingerly the deadly pill that floated, lobbying hard for active service, on a sea of cortisone and adrenaline somewhere beneath my tongue. Was this the right time to bite into it? I wasn't sure. Is there ever a good time to cross over to the other side of the river? No – don't answer that question. Not now. Not yet. 'On what grounds, may I ask?'

'You may not ask,' said bandana man – a reformed aesthete, for my money, having a sensitive mouth, and a duelling scar below one eye. 'Don't you get it? If you need to ask, you'll never know.'

Some of these people retain a sense of humour – an indulgence denied the rest of us under pain of two, or even three, civic penalty points depending on the severity of the offence. 'Do I have time to pack a bag?' I asked the black shirted master of ceremonies. 'A few items of comfort for the journey ahead, perhaps? The road is long that leads from sinfulness to salvation –'

'Two minutes,' barked the commandant before lapsing into a type of barrack-room or parade-ground argot intended, no doubt, to unsettle me further. '*Rangez vos affaires, et suivez-nous.*'

They came for me at midnight, the hour favoured by reluctant suicides and orphaned songbirds. I had my end-it-all capsule in my mouth – it could hardly have been readier for duty. Was I, perhaps, overreacting? I was new to all this derring-do. Yes, my general-issue cyanide formulation (this time-honoured methodology is yet to be bettered according to those who would still use it) came and went on my tongue like a curse or a prayer or a half-remembered name. The small and lethal tablet, its protective shell just delicate enough to suggest a child's vitamin supplement, I chose not to deploy in the moment of maximum jeopardy. Am I a hero or a coward? Of your midnight suicides designate I am possibly the most reluctant. As for the half-remembered names – lord, let us not overlook them. These names must one day save us from the fire.

On the landing outside my flat I popped the obvious question. 'Where are you taking me at this godforsaken hour of the night?'

'To the house of arraignment, of course.'

'Naturally, you are. Silly me. Guilty until proven innocent – at least you know where you stand with such a motto above the door.'

'Hurry up, hurry up —' exhorted an armed fanatic of seventeen summers from the top of the stairs. 'We ain't got all day, *book hugger.*'

'Allow me to close up my apartment,' I said, 'before we set out on our little adventure. This whole neighbourhood is going to the dogs, or very likely the wolves, and no mistake —'

'Don't waste your time,' advised the man with the red kerchief, waving his pistol eloquently in the general direction of eternity. 'Do you suppose you'll be coming back here any time soon?'

It was ten after twelve. My token suitcase was empty except for the framed photograph of K— on which I insist. Yes, I have been, within self-prescribed limits, a sentimentalist. (Please reject this idea of a black and white photograph. Such a relic doesn't exist — it never did. The past is off limits, all trappings deleted or denied.) The light flickered in the hallway and went out. Only the canteen of purified water strapped across my chest and over my tweed jacket gave me succour as our party descended grimly towards the front door and the street. (Water, believe me, is everything in a dry year. A flagon of the good stuff is all I carry with me from this world into the next.) At the foot of our communal stairwell a door opened suddenly, and there stood Samuelson, as promised earlier, in striped pyjamas and oversized dressing gown with a yellow light behind his head. *'Alles in Ordnung,* officers?' he enquired unctuously, all the while regarding my suitcase furtively. Abruptly, he made his move. 'Let me relieve you of that burden,' he said, lunging at the suitcase and spiriting it away between his legs in a single action. 'The thing is — I don't think you'll need it where you're going.' Here he let out a giggle, nodding wildly while rubbing his mitts like Lady Macbeth.

Then a most regrettable thing happened. The stray cat I had taken in just two weeks earlier made an unscheduled appearance in Samuelson's doorway before wrapping its body around my ankle in a rhombus of light. Within seconds the unfortunate creature was dead. Two shots rang out. 'No pets!' shrieked the sensitive chief of staff, swatting smoke from the tip of his Luger. 'Kitties *verboten* −'

Now a fluffy corpse lay tragically at my feet, and there was a smear of black blood on my shoe. I felt bad about the cat. To me, it represented an idea − no, a simple ideal − of the future. No doubt this was all bound up with the loss of K−. I had lost my best friend, and now I had lost my home. I felt sad − this is true. I knew I would have to rally if I was to do what I had to do. And still there was the important question of whether I would live to see another day.

'*Alles gut, ja?*' Samuelson summarised fawningly, wringing his hands in a show of deep feeling.

'Go back to bed, gramps,' urged a daughter of the ultras. 'And take your furry friend with you.'

OK − WHAT DO YOU WANT TO FIND OUT? I MEAN − how much do you need to learn in order to go about your business or to fulfil your mission? These days we operate strictly on a need-to-know basis − to do differently is to court betrayal and death. We live in a dream − think of it as a near-future dystopia. Officially, we have no books (you probably suspect this much already). We are bookless in Gaza, at the mill with slaves. Officially, we have no past. In truth, we have *keine Zukunft* − no future − either. We have no names, no religions, no interpersonal telecommunications, no taxes, no reliable rubbish collection, no pets, no bots − we exhibit many of the best narrative tropes, in other words. Specifically, we have no gods and no idols, false or otherwise. My handle is Oscar. I have my alphanumerical designation, of course, but I choose to be intimate with you today. How else will I persuade you to view this testament as more than the ravings of a mad person of the fledgling twenty-second century

AD? Good grief – did I say *AD*? Cut me down *now* with your light-amplification-by-stimulated-emission-of-radiation gun. What else? Discreet friends call me O–. In fact, I have no *other* type of friend – they are all either dead or disappeared. I am aged twenty-seven, a rebel by vocation, a home-maker by zodiac sign. I like knitting and soft furnishings. Oh, yes – and we find ourselves once again brutally oppressed by ultra-fascists in thrall to history deniers and born-again Nietzsches. The rest you'll discover soon enough.

My supper – he christened it the *last* supper – with Samuelson and his passionate wife was routine in most respects. 'Tonight's the night,' the old man told me before repeating this timely advice for the benefit of his new friend, my cat. 'Tonight's the night, Felix. Do you know what Felix means, O–? It means contented, or something close to it. Get happy, Felix. It's not so difficult, is it? You have only to uncover the ideal value of everything under the sun. But if you can't be happy, be lucky. This will get you there in half the time.'

On the table were three barbequed fish of dubious provenance (I didn't ask), plus a modest selection of misshapen vegetables whose black-market origin I took for granted. A crocheted doily had pride of place at the centre of our little feast – here stood a jug of water, respectfully small, and three tiny goblets. It was a little after seven o'clock when we finished hiding the last of my history books below the floorboards of the downstairs apartment in damp-proof sacks of many sizes, these prophylactics scavenged opportunistically by Mrs Samuelson from the rank landfill in Golders Green. As soon as we sat down, Samuelson reeled off an improvised grace that had to do with meagre rations and fellow travellers, while the cat, distracted by the presence of what passed in those days for fish, and exercised by a new responsibility for happiness, prowled from one set of feet to another just out of sight below our humble spread.

'Trust no one –' insisted Mrs Samuelson, homing in as always on what mattered most and seizing my arm across the table before she'd so much as lifted a fork. 'Promise me, Oscar – promise you'll follow your head only.' As her sleeve rode up I could see – we could all see – the old ID number stencilled crudely on her wrist beside today's stigmatising bar codes. She looked, to my eyes, a good deal younger than her spouse – how they met and fell in love during the first insurrection would soon become a cornerstone of legend. Even now she was, is, constantly disappearing, as in *going underground*, for weeks at a time, for reasons unspecified, to ends undisclosed. Never apologise, never explain – such was her guarded method in life, she told me, after I once invited her to account for these absences. Her scant frame – this is what I carry with me of Mrs Samuelson – was rocked at irregular intervals by involuntary tremors, as if subject to alternating electric current or the cruel attention of an unspeakable recall. 'Blessed are the pure in heart,' she went on intently now, as if to articulate an evangelical impulse all her own, voice rising, grip tightening, her silver-streaked hair sallying forth in every direction from her scalp. 'No harm will come to them – neither in this world nor the next. They are untouchable, O–. And why not? They shall see God, we are told. Let's just hope they report back soon –'

'Oscar's heart *is* pure,' Samuelson affirmed tolerantly, pouring three miniscule measures of water with low-key reverence into our glasses for the toast. 'Isn't that why he's been chosen?'

I wish I hadn't been chosen. Let's get that straight right away. I blame myself. This affair only started when I asked Samuelson to help me locate K–. I had always assumed my downstairs neighbour was a type of agent of the secret police. How else could he know the things he knew? Thus, it was a calculated risk I took. I don't regard myself as brave – that is for others to judge. I knew what I needed to do, and that is all. Our best people are disappearing, Samuelson confirmed, with his resistance hat squarely on. He told me he could help me, provided I was prepared to help him. He told me he knew a way, but the way was dangerous. Your wife, I said, has the habit of telling me to trust no one. How do I know I can trust you? When I put this question to the husband, he failed to answer directly. My wife is rather excitable, he said. She has her own faith and her own reasons. Moreover, she is inordinately fond of you, young man. I ask you only this – what would you give to find the one you love?

The supper plates had been pushed aside and the candle stubs had burned down. Mrs Samuelson excused herself temporarily in order to feed the mewling cat a few leftover scraps – now there was just me and the older man at the table in the downstairs flat.

'Will you take anything with you tonight?' Samuelson enquired significantly after a long silence.

'Only a likeness of K—,' I told him. 'It's all I have worth saving – apart from my books.'

'Your books are safe here,' Samuelson came back. 'If you want my advice, take with you nothing at all.' Here, he nodded, as if this question of the framed photograph was settled to his satisfaction. 'Under the bridge at midnight –' he added obscurely after a further brief hiatus. 'Let this be a mark or a sign of something unshakeable or immutable between us from now on.'

'I beg your pardon,' I offered conventionally, my heart beating a shade faster. *Under the bridge at midnight* – to me it had the qualities of a password exchanged by heroes engaged in desperate acts.

'Say it for me now, Oscar – tonight. Let me hear you say these few words which will bind us together for all time. If only you knew it – you are entering a profound darkness. Always remember – you are not alone. We are with you. You are never alone.'

At the door he kissed me twice and told me the goons would come for me at twelve o'clock sharp. As I say – that he was a police informer, and thus a kind of double agent, was a given as far as I was concerned. What did it mean? What did it mean for me? I had a mission of sorts – its terms and conditions were hopelessly vague. Our best operatives were disappearing left, right and centre. I was to go behind the lines and *find things out*. That was pretty much it in terms of the brief from Samuelson. Although I had a glimpse from moment to moment of the workings of his mind, I couldn't be quite certain of what he stood for, or to what he owed his true allegiance. I knew one thing – I was entering the lions' den. The stakes could scarcely be higher. Unless they could find a use for me, I would be a dead man by morning. If I woke up tomorrow, on the other hand, it would mean I had Samuelson's protection, for what it was worth. I couldn't see beyond these basic insights or assumptions. Such was the extent of my innocence, or ignorance, on this night of nights.

Suddenly, she was beside him in the doorway with the golden light behind her. She thrust it into my right hand – a small canister in the shape of a lipstick or a rifle round.

'The tablet inside this holder,' she began breathlessly, 'is your insurance policy. Rattle the charming pill box, Oscar. But carefully – so, so carefully. Can you hear it? Oh, yes. Here resides your exit strategy, the final solution. There can be no mistake about this. *Alles klar?* Do you understand what I'm telling you? Be sure to hide this crucial container where they can't find it. Imagine you stand – no, kneel – naked before me. What is it you fear most at this moment? There is nothing they won't do to break you, to confront you with your debased self. Though they abuse and humiliate you for their sport, spitefully, hatefully, and though they tear out your hair and teeth –' Here, she pulled back her cheek harshly with her finger to

139

expose the vacant lots on the ridges of her gums. 'Though they rip the heart – yes, the *pure* heart in Oscar's case – from your shattered body, yet they cannot rob you of your spirit or your soul. My dear boy – kindly pardon these incontinent ramblings. Believe me when I say I think only of you this midnight.' Then she peeled off a gold crucifix she wore around her neck and wound up the chain quickly and pressed the whole thing into my left hand and closed my fingers tightly around it.

'I can't take that,' I gasped, greatly affected by what she said and what and did. Slowly, I unclenched my fist to reveal the object gleaming dully there. Now I saw it featured the figure of Christ in tarnished silver. To me it looked beautiful and exceptional – three tiny jewels represented the nails of the forbidden story. What was it to be? A lucky charm? A bargaining chip? 'You know I can't accept such a precious talisman,' I told Mrs Samuelson, shaking my head for emphasis. 'Not from you. Not from anyone –'

'Ah, but you can,' she whispered. 'You can and you must. One day it may save someone's life.'

Abruptly, she was gone – swallowed, so to speak, by the light. My host nodded in the doorway, as if to indicate this chapter was now ended. Just then the bell began to toll in the old church of St Michael, long closed to worshippers, at nearby Wood Green. For what seemed like half a lifetime we two regarded each other without comment from either side of the threshold. (Had I known then what I know now I'd have lingered even longer there.) It was ten o'clock. 'Is it, perhaps, time to shred those documents of yours?' Samuelson asked after the bell fell silent. As I made my way up the stairs I felt his eyes on my back. When I reached the landing I heard him call out my number, or the start of it – this as a nod to discretion. 'Count on me at twelve,' he said. 'In case you change your mind –'

EVERYONE KNOWS THE HOUSE of arraignment. I mean everyone knows *of* it. Everyone (privately at least) acknowledges its location, tucked away in a complex of abandoned factories and requisitioned offices which the department of domestic security has called home since the halcyon days of the first insurrection. Two decades on, the department and its sprawling correction facilities are still very much here, sucking the vestigial oxygen from a post-industrial wilderness on either side of the poisonous superhighway, three lanes wide and as many storeys high, that girdles our consumptive city like a noose around its throat. Everyone recognises the existence of the house of arraignment here at the northern extremes of the metropolis. These days we call it quite simply the house of death.

Now we were close. A shifting of gears, followed by a palpable uplift in body temperatures within our wagon, marked the change. What was it Samuelson said? *You are entering a profound darkness.* As our bevy of transporters drew up, sirens caterwauling madly, at the revolving doors to the former budget hotel, I had reason to doubt the old boy's assessment of a few hours earlier. Night had become triumphant day. All was excoriating light in the reception zone of the house of death.

From the start I had several pressing issues on my mind. These were material factors – they had to do with sundry objects and their practical ramifications in the context of my detention. The flask of water I always took with me to the factory and on which I depended daily was virtually empty, its contents shared out scrupulously and ritualistically among my male companions – a sorry assortment of mostly harmless and blameless felons of terrified aspect – inside our unhappy wagon. I say male. In fact, there was a single exception to this rule – a calm and effortlessly dignified young woman (as I then thought) who had closely-cropped, lice-resistant hair and eyes the colour (as I then imagined) of the sky in August, and who refused my proffered flask with a casual exceptionalism.

Did I mention material issues? These distracted me massively, which wasn't necessarily a bad thing. Next on my menu of concern was a certain crucifix fashioned in precious metals and gemstones, and given to me in emotional circumstances. So far beyond the pale was this forbidden object that I had the idea it was plainly visible from outer space even as it burned a comforting hole in my chest beneath my shirt with its fire. So much for the cross of Jesus – the truth is I didn't know what to do with it. For a moment I considered simply consigning it to a heathen darkness below the benches of our jolting paddy-wagon. This option I rejected on moral and aesthetic grounds. For a transformative instant I had before me the shining eyes of Mrs Samuelson. Immediately, I knew what to do. I would wear the cross around my neck as she did, as she would have done here and now with the house of arraignment in the offing. The cross must guide me. This cross must save me, or else show me how and when to die. What else could it be for? (It is clear I clutched here at straws, as any drowning man will do. Although I am not, at bottom, a religious type, I am ready to entertain the notion of miracles in so far as they impact on my ability to endure or survive torture.) That only left the pill box and, of course, the pill itself – such a small thing to have such game-changing consequences in its gift. In respect of these paired items, their functionalities and destinies interlinked, I knew just what I had to do. Without a second thought I popped the freighted container into my mouth, added there the dregs from my trusty flask, and swallowed hard. Abruptly, the doors of our stinking wagon clattered open, and the pitiless light poured in.

Out! Out! Out! Such was their welcoming cry, followed almost immediately by another. *In! In! In!*

In the ground-floor lobby we were segregated, according to a hidden design, into groups of five or six. It was impossible to know in those first disorientating moments that these small groupings lent themselves ideally to a supervised bout of Russian roulette – all that, and much more, came later in the programme. For the time being it was sufficient to be alive and in one piece – astonishing how low one's expectations can sink from hour to hour. And yet there was sweetness here in the lobby as well as the superabundant light (this from four big searchlights that strafed the interior and the forecourt immediately beyond it in response to unscripted movements). The piped music was nice. There were actually plants in pots here. Can you believe that? There were some jarring notes, of course. Nothing is perfect. It was hard not to notice the primary installation – a fully functioning guillotine on loan from our friends across the water – at the centre of the light-lashed space. Around the walls at intervals, glass cabinets offered up a selection of carefully curated exhibits – garottes, thumbscrews, and so on. In a corner below the inevitable injunction to *abandon hope* stood an iron maiden with door open for inspection and spikes tipped with dye. That was a clever touch.

They say the beasts went in two by two. We did likewise. I was paired with my new girlfriend from the paddy-wagon, and that was OK by me. There was something about her disposition, which was cool but not cold, and her demeanour, which was sceptical and at the same time engaged, that told me everything I needed to know without having to ask. She was a rebel. She was one of us. She had to hose me down with cold water after our clothes were taken away from us, and I returned the favour. (If there was a shortage of sacred H_2O in our country, or indeed the world, you wouldn't know it in these unholy parts – more on that later.) This whole business of the hosing down is such a cliché, isn't it? Nothing really changes. With my new friend hopping naked in front of me I was obliged to adjust my sense of a nascent understanding between us. *She* was in fact *he*, and in an emphatic way besides. It was just one of several surprises to move my spirit from hour to hour in the cathedral of correction. Nevertheless, I was right about the eyes, which were of a cornflower blue, an uncompromising blue. Now the hackneyed hoses ran dry on us and our bracing *pas de deux*.

'O–,' I said by way of introduction, shivering freely with arms wrapped around my chest.

'O?' he said interrogatively by way of reply, jumping up and down with hands shielding his groin.

'O–,' I repeated, jabbing an identifying finger at myself in a helpful way.

'Oh,' he said, the penny dropping at last. '*B*.'

'Ah,' I said. 'B–. That's easy enough to remember.'

Finally, it was settled between us. My new friend advanced and confronted me at close quarters and peeled my arms from my chest. 'What in hell's name is that archaeological relic doing around your scrawny neck?' he enquired. 'Don't you know there's a *law* against wearing vintage nonsense like that?'

I don't remember very much about my first, my only, day in the house of death. Memory is a highly selective attribute, of course. It could be it is all still in there – it just hasn't found the right time to come out. No need to dwell unduly on the preliminary stages of my visit here, a painful merry-go-round of bare rooms, scrubbed corridors and humming elevators all of which had to do with acts of low-level violence involving electric shocks with bastinado, and designed, I supposed, to soften me up for what would happen next. (They told me later all this was a necessary smokescreen, it being essential to turn the screws on me in order to keep up appearances.)

As for their choice of a former budget hotel, with its endless parade of bedrooms of uniform size and specification – it was inspired. A democracy of terror flourished here – behind each partition a small world, within every world a small scream. All this time I considered the precocious pill and its holder buried inside me. There could be no prospect of revisiting these specialist items for days. Meanwhile, I tried not to dwell on the precious photograph that Samuelson had wrested from me using an otherwise empty suitcase at the eleventh, or twelfth, hour. What exactly was his game? I didn't know. I only knew my portrait of K– was gone – missing, as it were, in action. I could tell you a lot more about K–, of course. I could describe how we met and fell in love in the long shadow of the first insurrection, but what good would that do? Such stories are ten a penny.

I was standing in a cage. The cage was lowered repeatedly into a swimming pool at its deep end. Have I mentioned their profligacy with water? At intervals the cage was winched from the pool before being returned to the depths, with these intervals – above or below the surface – varying in line with an unpleasant metric. As the time spent above the surface decreased, the time spent below increased – all this in small and horrifying increments. I have never been a swimmer. I have seen the sea just once, and I don't remember what it looked like, far less felt like on the skin. Soon after I blacked out, I was happy. I was beside a great ocean in the company of K–. We were swimming towards what I took to be an abandoned lighthouse on a rock. This was at night. At some point I became separated from my friend. When I looked back, I couldn't see the shore.

Now I came round. Funny – I had assumed I was dead. In fact, I was only half-dead. I had closed down as far as possible any sense of myself, this in the interests of self-preservation. I was strapped at wrist and ankle to a chair in the middle of a white room which had a large window on one side. A few yards in front of me was a metal table with two young goons slouching half on and half off it. I had on a plain, ill-fitting garment – a kind of artist's smock in cotton or calico. There was daylight, a lot of it, in this room. I thought I was alone here with the guards, but I wasn't.

'Your ID number, please,' said a disembodied voice, a man's voice, from directly behind me. 'No, don't try to turn around. Don't look back, eh? Never look back – that's the style.'

Suddenly, it came to me – this vision of the cross of Jesus. Was it there? Was it still there around my neck? It had to be – there was no other way. Though I couldn't feel the cross, I knew it was there.

'Fear not,' said the voice uncannily. 'Your holy trinket is intact – as of now, at least. For the record, it's clear that man created God, rather than the other way round. Meanwhile, your number is?'

'WF57463294ZX –'

'That's terrific. It has a nice ring to it, doesn't it? And I bet it's easy to remember, too, O–. Do you mind if I call you Oscar, O–? No? Top man. Let's get down to business, then, shall we? Have you ever been a member of a proscribed organisation?'

'Nope.' This was, strictly speaking, a lie in a world where *any* form of association was suspect.

'Have you ever tested positive for SARS, or MERS, or HIV, or any of those tiresome acronyms?'

'Of course not.' In general, my replies were designed to strike a note of righteous indignation.

'Are you an active invert, Oscar? Are you what might be called a practising – we don't really need to *say* it, do we? Well – are you?'

'Do me a favour –'

We have always been persecuted, haven't we? We have always been reviled. Let fashions and seasons come and go – some things

146

never change. There came a double slap, as from a pair of leather gloves, against the back of my head and the side of my face. 'Think carefully, my friend,' said the voice. 'We know more about you than you could possibly imagine. If it was down to these sexual saboteurs we would rapidly die out as a species, would we not? There would be nothing left of us or our project of social renewal. I repeat – are you a practising deviant, or aren't you?'

'I have no time to practise anything. I'm extremely busy at the factory making uniforms and prison issue. The excellent garment I have on now – I may even have stitched it myself.'

'Oh? No time to practise a little book-binding of a long winter's evening? Such a pity, Oscar. Let me remind you of the facts. Books are dangerous and unnecessary. Books – especially history books – are inimical to progress. Why dwell on the past, eh? What good will it do at the end of the day?'

Here, there was pause. Abruptly, the two guards snapped to a kind of attention, as if in response to a signal. 'God is dead!' they cried in unison, saluting before exiting at pace. From beyond and below the picture window came a ragged volley of gunshots.

'Pay no attention,' advised the voice behind me airily. 'That's just the firing squad warming up.'

There were to be no experimental truth serums today, and no torture. They wanted – no, expected – me to enter their maximum rehabilitation programme, to follow it as far as it would take me, up to and including the bitter end. That was the deal. In return I would avoid execution for my crimes, or sins.

'We've been leaking traitors and dissidents like the proverbial,' explained the voice. 'It reflects rather badly on me. Key detainees, once processed, have escaped our reach in embarrassing numbers. How do they manage it, these gypsies, Jews and queers? We want you to find out. It's really no more complicated than that.' Here, a second barrage of shots rang out dismally. 'Beware, Oscar. Others have gone before you, only to fail in colourful circumstances, their throats slit with a rusty scythe, their guts the reward of badgers. And don't imagine we won't be watching you. Though we love you as a prodigal son, we are always ready to terminate your contract, and, indeed – let's not be coy here – you too. Now, do you accept our generous offer or not?'

'How will I report back to you?'

'Oh, I dare say you'll find a way. Our sources describe you as focused and enterprising.'

'Sources?'

'Yes, naturally – *sources*.' Now the straps at my wrists and ankles were removed. 'Have you ever witnessed an execution by good old-fashioned firing squad, my boy? No? You're in for a treat.'

In the courtyard – once a hotel car park – below our window, nine men stood in a line wearing shapeless vestments with backs to the pockmarked wall. They all looked pretty much the same, these nine, with their dun clothes and shaved heads – that was the terrible thing about it. They all looked the same, with one exception. The man second from the right as I looked down on the courtyard had refused the blindfold. This individual – number two or eight – I recognised with a sharp jolt. After I started banging on the glass of the window he looked up defiantly with his piercing blue eyes. I had a real chance here. I had an opportunity to face down destiny, and I seized it with both hands. 'I accept your offer,' I said, coming alive finally, 'on one condition. That man down there –'

'Oh, but how perfectly charming and touching –' enthused the masked general beside me while patting my buttocks negligently. 'I knew we could count on your fine judgement.'

'I do believe,' I said, 'a bright future lies ahead of us. Just don't touch me ever again —'

I WAS A SPY. CORRECTION — I WAS DOUBLY A SPY. If I was twice a spy, then I was also two times a traitor. It was funny and absurd. On the one hand, I appeared to have attracted co-sponsors implacably opposed to each other's brand. On the other, I served twin masters who, in all probability, knew I acted for both of them. Better still — I was charged by two parties with fulfilling exactly the same mission on either side of their ideological divide. Yes, I was to *find things out*. If it was a game, it was a game without rules. It was comical enough, but also risky. Someone, somewhere, expected it — and me — to end badly. Meanwhile, if I was on both sides, I was on neither, or none. I was doubly expendable, twice disavowed. Who would claim my body from the battlefield? Then I saw it — in a moral jungle I must fashion my own rules. If staying alive involved playing this side off against that, so be it. Nevertheless, I felt dirty. Then it came to me — why not let scheming Samuelson be my guide? *What would you give to find the one you love?* Isn't that what he once asked me? If it was the right question then, it was an even more potent one now, loaded as it increasingly was with kindred notions of death and desire.

It was true that Samuelson was still very much beside me. You had to hand it to the old boy — it was a masterstroke to market the idea the way he did. It was almost as if he was standing, had once stood, in my shoes with the same conflicted feelings in his heart. He got it — he understood. If I was doing this for love, that was OK — any amount of shame or degradation was acceptable. That was the price of the ticket. There was only one drawback, wasn't there? As you were — there was only one snag having multiple offshoots and bifurcations. It had everything to do with the photograph I held so dear. As each moment passed without this physical reminder in my hand, the memory I held of K– receded further in my imagination. This caused me pain, and also alarmed me. What if my recollection should disappear altogether, and love with it? The greater problem, however, was tactical. How far was I likely to get in my sentimental search if I was unable to share a likeness of K– in this lousy corner of the world or that? Matter arising – had Samuelson hijacked the picture expressly to scupper my quest? Why would he do that? We were friends, weren't we, as well as allies or co-conspirators? What was a rookie spy to think? I was at a loss. I couldn't see the pathway ahead. Only one thing could rescue me – of this I was convinced. I had to hold the photograph in my hand again. Without it there was no mission as such – not really. I was a pawn in their brutal game. No cross of Jesus would save me from myself. Such a pity, then, that my options for recovering the fateful portrait in its frame numbered less than zero at this disconcerting time.

The stadium, rotting, unsafe, was in the top righthand corner of the city as you looked at the map. Designed half a century ago as a multi-use sports venue, it had found itself playing host across the turbulent decades since to grazing cattle, horses at stud, rabbits in cages, and lambs for slaughter. Animal husbandry aside, its credits included a spell as an execution facility in the worst years of the first insurrection. Today, it served as a transit station for people like me – fortunate individuals embarking on the maximum rehabilitation programme. We were all here in a sunblasted stadium – the gypsies, the Jews, and the queers. Oh, and B– was here too. I wasn't sure which of these three categories, if any, he belonged to. He was with me now. I had recently saved him from the executioner's bullet.

'What can ail thee, secret agent,' he enquired allusively, 'alone and palely loitering? Look around you, Oscar. Hell is other people.'

All day long the transporters had been drawing up at the doors to discharge their human cargo, and now the stadium was full. I say full – the parched floor was crammed with the old and infirm, their black umbrellas raised, their possessions gathered around them in pitiful bundles. The tiered terraces that rose at an incline all around from ground level were the dominion, filled to capacity, of the able-bodied. Above these, stretched out in attitudes of repose in order to distribute their weight as evenly as possible, the fittest of us – young men, mostly – colonised the flimsy canopies of corrugated iron that topped the perimeter of the structure. Just before nightfall the word went about – we were part of a new wave, a novel tide of correction and realignment. Then they shut the big doors and locked them.

Nothing of significance occurred that night in the hellish bowl – unless, that is, you countenance the baby. I am talking here about Blue and myself. (B– is now Blue. When I asked him what the letter B stood for, he told me it didn't stand for anything – it had no real meaning. He was the second of three boys called, he explained, for ease of reference, A, B and C.) In terms of the wider population of our fetid enclosure, it is fair to say that *everything* had significance – that is, everything was reduced in very short order to the level of the most basic needs. Food and water were scarce. No surprise that scuffles broke out from time to time as partisan groups bartered or otherwise vied for what victuals existed. And there were no working toilets inside the stadium. Within hours our palace of confinement became an open sewer. Soon the filth was running from the terraces to the plateau below. Our misery was, in the purest sense, olfactory. When they closed the big doors, they did so to shut in the stench.

In the midnight hour I was curled up beside Blue on a sliver of more or less dry ground towards the middle of the stadium. Sleep was impossible, at least for the adults. From all directions came the confused alarms – intermingled cries, prayers and prophecies – of hungry, frightened people. I remember clearly there being a fullish moon – it cast a subtle and merciless half-light upon us, registering our misfortune in the most delicate tones of silver and gold. In such a situation, anything might happen. At such a time, nothing is too extreme. There was a girl or a young woman lying on her back on the other side of Blue, which is to say she was very close to us. This woman had a baby – I mean she delivered herself of a child without us knowing until the last moment. Perhaps the mother abandoned hope – she died in silence immediately after giving birth, with the bawling baby still attached to her. Blue attended impassively and impressively to the needs of the hour. Kneeling at the scene, he first closed the mother's eyes, then drew forth a short knife I had never seen before and cut the baby loose.

'Where did you discover that handy little blade?' I asked him straight off.

'Does it matter?' he replied. 'I had to commit a lewd act to get my hands on it.'

'Well, now – is it an orphaned boy or an orphaned girl we have in our company tonight?'

'It's a girl, just like its mother once was. The question is – what are we going to do with her, Oscar?'

'That's a tough call, it seems to me, regardless of which female you refer to. The context – it could hardly be less favourable.'

After we composed the body as decently as we could, we spent a good deal of time begging for water with which to wash the new-born baby. With every enquiry we made we were looking to donate our screaming bundle to a good home (our principal preoccupation was, understandably, with the spying game). No such home existed that night. A mother of three who offered to share her breast milk with us said our baby, sound asleep now in strong arms, would be dead by dawn. I saw no reason to contest her view. But Blue, highly motivated by a powerful instinct, would have none of it.

'I will save this baby,' he decreed boldly, raising the infant girl towards an indifferent heaven. 'I will rescue this motherless child, or die trying.'

'There shall arise false Christs and false prophets,' warned an interested believer on wooden crutches.

'The Antichrist is coming,' insisted a second witness, wrestling with Blue for possession of the baby.

'He will be a Jew like you,' added a third. 'A Jew from the tribe of Dan, for thus it is written.'

These unwarranted and unwelcome interventions were cut off by a crackling sound, incredibly loud, from a public address system no one had noticed until now. We were to prepare ourselves for a journey – so we were told by a soothing voice, a voice practised at corporate communications. We should look forward to a brave new chapter in our wretched lives. Privileged and special, we were set to populate a series of labour camps in the north, digging fields for the empire, sowing seeds for the empire, and growing crops for the sons and daughters of the empire. It would be the highwater mark – yes, the culminating point – of our experience. It was fundamental work for which we had been individually chosen, that is to say *hand-picked*. This work would begin without delay. This work would set us free.

'We're all going to die,' someone argued shrilly on behalf of a sceptical tendency. 'Don't you get it? They're going to slaughter us one by one and feed us to the fishes.'

For a moment following this outburst there was a discouraging silence in our stadium. Just then the sun poked its head above the iron roof on the east side. After ten seconds or so, several hundred children began to wail in eerie unison. Soon the great doors swung open magically and the first transporters drew up outside. *Out! Out! Out!* A great mass surged forward blindly. *In! In! In!*

I WAS ON A JOURNEY NORTH. MY FRIEND BLUE was beside me, his as yet unnamed child (the idea of this capable young man becoming the girl's adoptive father had taken hold naturally) tucked inside his plaid shirt. I had never been to the north. Like the ocean, it existed in my imagination as something mythical and mystical, or at least lyrical. It was better than the south, was it not? It was much wetter, for a start. It was less ravaged by the mistakes of the past, its people faithful to an ideal of independence and freedom from the usurper's yoke. This is what I chose to believe as we lurched painfully towards New Glasgow and towards our fate. Hope is a mirage in a desert of illusion, and a cherished fantasy is still just a fantasy.

I want to give you some idea of the scale of our migration, our enforced pilgrimage. By the time the first carriages of our departing train reached the outer suburbs of the capital, the rearmost wagon was only just leaving the inner zone. Such is my best estimate, based on what I saw later. Where was I within this crawling caravan – at the front, at the back, or somewhere in the middle? It didn't matter. Our shameful exodus had no meaningful shape or form. It was an idea inside a notion within a dream – a gospel practised, perfected and patented in hell. Inside these myriad cattle wagons, however, human existence was at its most current, vivid and physical. I won't detain you with the sad details. A few brushstrokes will often sum up the scene. Suffice to say that when someone died, typically but not exclusively from asphyxia, he or she lingered awhile, propped up by weight of numbers, before being consigned, after a respectful interval and by tacit agreement, to a floor of trampled suitcases and the grace of God. What we learned on that sordid express train – it was as nothing compared to the lessons that came after.

We crossed over dry rivers unknown. We snaked through cities unidentified or unrecognised. Every now and then a pathetic shout went up in the wilderness of our wagon. *Look – it's bloody Birmingham! Blimey – that's Liverpool, or I'm a Dutchman!* In due course we perfected a system of synchronised rotation around the interior of our reeking box so as to expose ourselves justly to a ribbon of air that teased the ventilation slots of its shell at eye level. In this way various bizarre or unsettling exterior facets of our journey presented themselves in an impressionistic or surrealistic tableau. I witnessed, for example, numberless instances of execution, recent or otherwise, of corpses swaying on ropes beneath the acacia trees, of bodies drooping and sagging in rows of twenty or more from the cross of St Andrew in a field of sugar cane or high on a hill. I saw a graveyard for planes – these decommissioned jets of every commercial marque stretched three or four deep, with tyres slashed and engines stripped, for miles beside us while the setting sun flashed from their looted cockpits.

Night fell heavily on us. I was thinking of my friend Blue, from whom I had become separated, and the baby he cradled within his shirt. Were they still with me, so near but so far away? Were they alive? I thought of the young mother we had left behind us – at that time I would have given a lot just to know her name. In a period of deathly quiet I called out to my friend with all my might. After what seemed like an age, I heard my own name float back to me on the feeble breath of the living. Everything was going to be fine, wasn't it? When I thought finally, dutifully, of my dear K– I felt a pang of guilt. Why? This emotion was quickly dispelled by actual forces.

There was a man standing, or something like standing, beside me. I mean there was a person of interest stationed very close, his body pressed against mine. That I knew this man came as a double shock to me. It was a shock first of all because the most basic act of survival in these degrading circumstances demanded an anonymity without compromise. The other factor had to do with the duelling scar I could just about discern high on the cheek above the sensitive mouth. What was he doing here, the kitten killer with the smoking Luger who arrested me in my flat half a lifetime ago? For an instant my mind raced and reeled. Our convoy halted with a shrieking of brakes. That is, it stopped *again*, only this time the heavy doors slid open with an appalling clatter. Those placed nearest the exit simply fell out of our wagon onto a bank of gorse that rose up from the side of the track. At the crest of the rise a line of armed goons stretched to left and right as far as the eye could see in the moonlight. Trust the moon to show up uninvited when the stakes were high – it could generally be relied on to turn the screw or twist the knife.

Now my scarred acquaintance kissed me harshly on the mouth before raising a flask and offering it to me at close range. It was my flask he held – that was the funny thing. It was my trusty flask, last seen at the house of death in a far-off city. I saw the crocodile clips and the electric probe. I heard the volley of gunshots. I glimpsed an abandoned lighthouse. These perceptions occasioned no joy – they served only to distract me from the questions at hand. In what way did scar man, ghost of my recent past, lay claim to my future? And what did he want with my faithful flagon? *Out! Out! Out!* Along the line the familiar cry went up. Scar man drained my flask, then held the thing upside down and empty in a type of metaphorical verdict on the state of the world. 'Welcome to Scotland,' he said.

ACT TWO
The Camp

THE FIRST THING TO SAY IS THAT WE were not the first. Ours was
not the first train to visit Caledonia with a cargo of undesirables and
unmentionables fit only for termination by any reasonable method.
Nor was ours the only camp of its kind in these hills and glens – not
by a long chalk. It was common knowledge among those of us who
carried on living that the machinery of murder was widely established
in this green and pleasant (unless the old guidebook plugs are to be
ignored altogether) land. There were the lawless towns and cities –
these might as well have been located in Outer Mongolia for all the
influence they exerted on our day-to-day existence. There were the
death factories – it is true that a modicum of organic farming took
place at or around these grisly sites, but the produce thus harvested
was destined only for the supper tables of the camp commandants.
And there were the forests, the few left untouched by the clearances
of yesterday. In these forbidden thickets lurked the partisans, led by
their warrior queen. That they lived in trees, and survived on nuts
and berries, we took for granted. At all times they were the subject
of rumour, prayer, conjecture and dream in our camp workshops
and dormitories. Hope here was otherwise in short supply.

Each morning after a meagre breakfast of bread with tea I took
up my position at the bench in my workshop – one of several utility

stations located at the centre of the site beside the armoury and the Nissen huts in which we slept, washed and ate. The extinction zone – strictly out of bounds to tourists on pain of summary execution – was at the southern extremity of the facility where the noblest trees of the forest threw long shadows across the perimeter fence towards us, as if reaching out with the consoling hand of oblivion. Those of us who worked at the site did so only by virtue of the declared skills and aptitudes, real or invented, which had saved us from immediate destruction and without which the programme of slaughter might grind to a halt from day to day or week to week. Our motley band of survivors included engineers, blacksmiths and carpenters – these worthy trades are fundamental to the smooth running of any death factory. Less obviously necessary were the jewellers. From hour to hour these talented craftsmen (to the best of my recollection they were all men) laboured to recast or to reconfigure such objects and materials of value as had been carried through the gates in leaking luggage, or, in the case of countless gold implants, ripped from the mouths of new arrivals during their last moments in this world.

There was one among our number whose designated role was to stitch or repair the garments that clothed the camp, and to design and manufacture soft furnishings in accordance with the tastes and whims of our supreme overlord and master. So it was that the camp commandant – precociously young, surely, for such responsibility, capricious and sadistic by reputation, and fanatical in the discharge of his official duties – held my particular fate in his soft hands. I say *soft*. Were they soft, these bloodstained hands? No one really knew, because the hands of the young commandant were rarely on view. Were they always gloved? Who could be certain of anything at all in respect of the mayor of murder? In his case the cult of personality grew in, or emanated from, the darkness. He was never seen in the everyday lanes and courtyards of the camp. Even so, his power was absolute. He was a king in a land without gods. To be his favourite, it was generally accepted, would be a terrible privilege.

Let me introduce you here to my fellow toilers – the half dozen or so jewellers and workers in metal who shared that stifling cabin warmed to an excessive degree by the smelting stoves and soldering irons of their trade. Many had travelled from across the water to be with us at this important time and in this remarkable place. All were understandably obsessed with the psychology and methodologies of execution at scale. These were creative people well used to allowing their imaginations free rein.

'I can't think what they do with all the bodies,' admitted Levi, putting the finishing touches to a signet ring commissioned by one of the Russian auxiliaries who enforced camp law on behalf of the ultras. 'I mean – if they burned those corpses in great big ovens, we would be able to smell them a mile off, wouldn't we?'

'This compound would stink to high heaven,' affirmed Aaron, holding an enormous diamond up to the light of the window using tweezers. 'On the other hand, they do say you get used to anything after long enough.'

This was on a typical morning early in our story. There were no days of the week here, and no weekends. Our faceless hours were marked out by the solemn tolling of a bell in the main courtyard of the camp. Meanwhile, only the slow shifting of the seasons glimpsed in the mutating hues of the forest betrayed the overarching progress of time. It was high summer in the heart of Scotland.

'In my view,' offered Cyclops, a big man so named in honour of the watchmaker's eyeglass he carried strapped to his magnificent forehead, 'their preferred method is simply to push you backwards off the nearest or highest cliff. Partisans permitting, of course –'

'Don't be absurd,' advised Daniel, strewing gold teeth across his bench from a pouch of chamois leather. 'That hardly amounts to a strategy, does it? In any case, you've failed to resolve the stink issue there. You're merely swapping one type of smell for another.'

'Not necessarily,' countered Cyclops reasonably. 'It depends if your cliff overlooks the sea, does it not? If so, the bodies are swept away towards Nuevo New York or Iceland by the next tide.'

'That's clever –' Daniel acknowledged. 'But not clever enough. What if the bodies were drowned in a freshwater loch first and then flushed far out to sea using a system of large bore tunnels?'

Now Levi cut across them angrily. 'You boys sound like you're celebrating or validating these diabolical ideas. Don't you know it, or have you merely forgotten it? These people are evil. Their work is the work of the devil. Or are we becoming more like them every day without realising it?'

The truth, of course, was more technical and less poetic than these fanciful scenarios allowed. The gypsies, Jews and queers were poisoned chemically in sealed chambers, their dead bodies carried day and night by rail to one of several dedicated incineration plants dotted around the countryside. Doubtless a tell-tale aroma could be linked to this round-the-clock endeavour, but only if the prevailing breeze was from the wrong direction. In point of fact, the reality of what took place inside the secret chambers at the southern limits of our camp was unknown to many of the guest workers. I refer here to the exact means or manner of execution. I myself only arrived at the truth when I stumbled by accident on a vast cache of Zyklon-B canisters stacked up like tins of baked beans in a locked storeroom.

The other two men in our cabin you know already. The fellow with the scarred face was here with us. His name was Frenchie. He came from Paris – or would have done, he said, if they hadn't razed the city to the ground years ago. Frenchie was my ultras minder, of course. Having quickly identified himself as an undercover agent of the goons using my faithful water bottle, his role was to keep an eye on me at all times. His mission, in other words, was to promote my mission. Why didn't he simply do my job for me? Such a question, which took me back to a world of electric shocks and firing squads and big decisions, wasn't really worth asking. If I wasn't spying, I'd be face down in a ditch or pushing up daisies – that was the bottom line. And Frenchie wasn't altogether bad, despite having executed my cat in another place. One of the helpful things he did here, very early on, was save my life.

That just leaves Blue. Yes, my best friend was still with me. He was still in this world rather than the next one. He wasn't, truth to tell, a jeweller by calling. He was only pretending to know all about gold and silver or diamond necklaces and brooches. Once again, it was Frenchie who made the case for Blue's life when the chips were down. Too bad the one with the scar was unable to save Blue's baby into the bargain. Today, I still want to believe the new-born girl was already dead when we entered the camp. How could such a fragile thing have survived the train journey from one hell to another? The sad fact was – my friend with the cobalt blue eyes hadn't said a word since that first morning. It was as though he had been struck dumb by what happened in the main courtyard during the processing and preparation of our ragged cohort for the gas chambers. Hadn't he vowed to save that little girl or die trying? Now it was as if he really had died back there. I too felt a kind of grief. Much of this was for the baby, of course, but the lion's share I reserved for my friend.

One more thing relating to this formative period is well worth mentioning right now. There existed in the camp an administrative hierarchy which, from top to bottom and bottom to top, managed every aspect of life from a domestic, as it were, point of view. There was even an office dedicated exclusively to this vital organisational apparatus. Based in the office from this shift to that was Benjamin S, a turncoat Jew whose altered allegiance had thus been rewarded in kind. I recall thinking it must have been difficult for Benjamin to sleep at night – no doubt he kept a knife under his pillow. It was to this office and this awkward youth that I reported with my mended clothes and my soft furnishings for the commandant's quarters. The first time I interacted with Benjamin he instructed me to make two square cushions stuffed with hair, by which he meant human hair. It was as I gradually came to terms with this distasteful order that a certain item caught my attention. On a shelf behind and above the quartermaster's head was my framed photograph of K–. It was just squatting there, as if all this was a natural state of affairs. I was about to cry out. Then I saw what was happening here. The photograph was a sign from Samuelson. Hadn't he snatched it away from me at the bottom of the stairs outside his flat? Now I saw why. He had a foothold, a presence, here. My working method was to say nothing to anyone about anything. Nevertheless, it was plain. Insiders acted covertly to make my mission, or missions, a success. I was immortal, untouchable. If I was on both sides, both must be on mine. 'Where do you keep the most recent human hair?' I asked young Benjamin S at that time. 'I want new hair, please – the fresher the better.'

'The human hair we keep in the non-perishable storeroom, as you'd expect. Now, can I trust you with my keys?'

THIS IS HOW IT HAPPENED. I PRESENT THIS documentary account without fear or favour, but, rather, in the spirit of a public enquiry that neither assigns blame nor infers guilt. We all have our reasons – in this they are as we are, and I am the same as you. Moreover, I am ever mindful of my precarious position as a double, or a *double* double, agent. It goes without saying that allegiances can be bought or sold. I am not speaking here of dollars or diamonds – in a killer's market, the promise of protection is the only currency worth having.

Imagine the scene. It is a moonlit night in the central lowlands of Scotland. The gorse bushes are in bloom – their brilliant yellow flowers throw a kind of secondary light on the open fields. *Out! Out! Out!* As we mill about – those of us who can still mill – on the incline that borders the railway track, the ultras descend the slope towards us in riot clobber, their submachine guns raised, their visors flashing coldly. At this time their chief interest lies not with those of us who stand. Their first priority is to silence the cries from the cattle trucks behind us of the not-quite-dead and the dying. Shots split the night for five seconds. (Have you ever been beside an active machine gun, or ten of them, say, or twenty? The racket alone is enough to stop your heart.) Those who are dying inside the wagons are soon dead. After the goons hop back down, the heavy doors slide closed on this most gruesome chapter of our lives. Now we have come home. The death train sails on towards a notional quay in a sea of poppies. The full moon wanes. This train never docks – it sails onwards forever.

I am in a snaking queue with the other men. This is just inside the main gates of the camp, which are flung wide to accommodate our volume and number. (There is a further group behind us, and a further group waiting patiently behind that one to take its turn. If I cite three hundred pilgrims, think of four or eight hundred. If I list one thousand participants, simply double that tally or treble it.) Beside us, the women are also marshalled in a line that bends back on itself many times. For some reason the women's line looks longer than our line. It is only when you separate people thus that certain demographic tendencies are revealed. For example, although there are more of them, the women seem older than the men. No doubt men die younger, carried off early by the great bird of despair. Just beyond the women is a third, shorter line. This is the line, silent and stoical, of older children. Beyond the older children, in a big cot on wheels, are the crawling toddlers and supine tots. These visionary infants also make no sound. It is as if they have already exchanged this life for a better one – a life of toys, say, or milk. If I look behind me, I can see trailers stacked with goods and chattels. Many of the suitcases here assembled have been breached, their spilled contents glistening, entrail like, in the raking sunshine.

At the head of each line – of men, of women, of children – is a trestle table with two functionaries sitting behind it. The welcome committee here includes a dozen or so armed guards – Russkies by racial profile – with a roaming brief and specially selected, it would seem, for their fierce aspect. I am second now in the queue of men. Directly behind me is the man with the facial scar. This fellow has remained doggedly by my side since we quit the railway track and the moonlit prairie under armed escort. A puppy could not be more faithful than this mystery man, who carries an empty water bottle strapped across his shoulder, and who also bears an ornate crucifix, torn from around my neck just one hour ago, in his clenched right hand. Behind the man with the scar is my best friend Blue. We are a team, we three, a family. We look out for each other, as brothers will. Soon our loyalties will be tested in an unforgettable way. But something else happens before that. To my right, at the head of the women's line, a guest remonstrates with a female functionary. This guest worker, a young woman of independent spirit, is determined to argue the toss at the welcome desk. What can possibly have gone wrong here? Perhaps the young guest worker lacks the skills needed to plough the fields and, later, to scatter the good seed on the land.

Perhaps she is constitutionally unsuited to a farmer's life, or the role of a farmer's wife. We don't know. We can't be certain at this time. Abruptly, Blue makes an intervention on the girl's behalf. 'Can you bake bread and cook?' he shouts. 'Can you make flowers grow?' In the ensuing silence the girl turns to confront Blue. 'Yes, I can,' she confirms in a cool, clear voice, before being dragged off by a leering Cossack. She will join an elite group behind the tables of those who refuse the hoe, this subset watched by a young officer, immaculately groomed, with swagger stick and toothbrush moustache.

They are looking for people with certain aptitudes. A cook can be useful – everyone knows that. A decent cook is of more use alive than dead. We only know they are not really interested in farming outcomes, in prize marrows and the like, because we – a select few of us – have been briefed accordingly by the man with the scar. We don't know where he gets his information from, but he is evidently on the inside track at all times. So it is that we know, Blue and I, or we think we know, how to behave at the trestle table.

'Next *Gastarbeiter*, please –' I am not sure I would have worked it out for myself. I don't know if I would have had the presence of mind to figure out what was happening. All around me the people were talking up their agricultural credentials or farming skills. Why wouldn't they, given what we'd been told by a mellifluous voice in a rank stadium? 'Good morning – your personal designation is?'

'A catchy WF57463294ZX. Let's exchange numbers when we get to know each other better.'

'Do you have any previous agricultural experience? No? Then are you a member of a horticultural society, by any chance?'

'Unfortunately, I have no experience in this important sphere. Nevertheless, I am super keen to support the sons and daughters of the empire in any way I can. Please tell me how I can serve.'

'What other transferable skills, if any, do you have to offer?'

'I sew. As a matter of fact, I stitch fast and well. Many people have commented favourably on my sewing skills – even people who don't know me and therefore have little to gain by flattering me.'

'Are you trying to be funny?' Now they are quietly laughing at me. Are they laughing at me or with me, and what is the meaningful difference between these two variables in the current context? 'Pass through, smart arse, and wait behind this table.'

I have made it as far as the other side. When I look back over my shoulder I see that Blue is now at the trestle table with scar man directly behind him. Why have they changed places? I don't know. I only know that Blue is, from this moment on, a practised jeweller and engraver. He looks to me nothing like a jeweller. Nevertheless, it is all going well for my young friend. He is preparing to cross over to the other side when something miraculous and terrible happens. *Stop! Wait!* What happens is this – the baby that was dead begins to cry. That's right – the infant lost beneath Blue's plaid shirt starts to whimper piteously. Immediately, Blue is confronted by the Cossack – yes, the same leering guard. What does he *want* with us, this pawn of destiny? The guard has a horrible job to do. He rips open Blue's shirt and takes out the baby and swings it around by its legs a few times above his head and then smashes the head down on the table repeatedly until the head splits open and becomes partly detached from the body. Within seconds, head and body lie under the trestle table at the feet of the clerks. There is a surprised silence. Blue lets out a howl the tenor of which is hard to describe. He has both hands at the Cossack's throat now. Doubtless he thinks of the handy little blade with which he once cut an umbilical cord. Too late – the chap with the scar is a quick-witted moderator at the fraught scene. After he manhandles Blue roughly to the ground, this chap embraces the

166

guard like a second cousin and whispers sweetly in a Cossack's ear. Something gleams dully in the sun as it passes from hand to hand between these two. What can it be if not the gold and silver crucifix complete with precious stones and chain?

'We're all going to die —' someone shrieks from the men's line. 'Don't you understand? They're going to strangle us one by one and then dissolve our bodies in acid.'

That is how we came, Blue and I, to be licensed workers at the death terminal in the heart of Scotland. The others didn't make it. They were marched, still dreaming of a life of the sod, to the killing zone at the southern edge of the site. Here, their heads were shaved and their mouths assessed by experts with pliers for items of value. A special touch this — they were given a towel each to preserve their modesty in preparation for the shower stations beyond the second set of doors. It was as they passed from the first to the second set of doors that these towels were taken from them without explanation or apology (such details I had later by the grapevine). Then, after a suitable interval, the inner doors slid shut noiselessly behind them.

THE DAYS SLIPPED PAST LIKE — WELL, like nothing on earth. There was just me and the camp and the suffocating logic of confinement. The universe was a rectangle measuring approximately one square mile and bounded on four sides by a perimeter fence of timber and barbed wire — part of a ditch-mound complex designed as much to keep the barbarian out, it seemed, as in. Where would we go? What we would escape to, if not the outlaw's life in a wintry wood and a permanent state of exile in the bosom of the partisans? And they — why would they choose to intrude on our discreet madness if not to gain access to the best stocked armoury in the territory? The camp existed to liquidate gypsies, Jews and queers. The guards, officers, and auxiliaries oiled the machinery of murder. In all this, the guest workers had a supporting role. Meanwhile, the partisans existed for no other reason than to oppose this satisfactory order both as a fact and an idea. Thus, a curious balance of forces and interests held in harmonious equilibrium the players and parties of our world.

It was my job to change that. This had nothing to do with my official mission, or missions, to uncover treachery wherever it might be found. No – it was for me to set fire to the sick house, to turn the world order here represented upside down, in so far as I could. How to do it? How to stay alive long enough to answer the call? I didn't know how to act. Such a heavy responsibility scared me. Its burden kept me awake at night. As I waited for a sign – a sign from God, if necessary – I began to see it. The message and the method and the means resided in the camp itself – that is, in its physical parameters and limitations. It was all about the logic of confinement. A hidden pattern would out. A structural blueprint would reveal its hand.

The compound took the form, as already noted, of a rectangle whose long sides faced west towards New Glasgow and east towards what was, once upon a time, Edinburgh. About half way along the western boundary were the main gates, flanked, as is traditional, by control towers, and approached via the road from the railway line. On either side of this access road, the trees of the forest – a riotous mixture of evergreen with deciduous types – had been cut harshly back to discourage ambush. The same road led, inside the gates, to the main courtyard, a floodlit clearing that served both as a parade ground for the garrisoned ultras, and the reception zone, active day and night, for processing the incoming hordes. Dotted around this central quadrangle were the workshops and sleeping quarters of the guest workers, plus a variety of storage facilities, including the large armoury. A refectory for officers and other ranks, and the kitchens, were also located here. At the southern part of the site, and circled about by their own interior palisade, were the gas chambers. It was obvious to me, having once arrived at the terrible truth about these sealed bunkers, that a phantom railway must exist for the purpose of taking the bodies to their final destination. How else to complete the job and get paid? Inside the northern perimeter of the site were the barracks for enlisted men, an officers' mess or recreation room, and the commandant's bungalow, this last erection an otherworldly habitation with south-facing veranda hosting a rocking chair and a sizeable kennel in wood. It was a mark of his degenerate tendency, so it was widely held, that our master-in-chief kept a dog, a German Shepherd, in defiance of his own prescription.

At around this time I was selected, with others from our group, for my first wood-cutting foray into the forest that abutted the camp on its southern flank. The wood was needed to fuel the incinerator, modest in size but epic in ambition, that toiled ceaselessly to dispose of the clothes discarded by the undesirables and unmentionables in the last moments before they went to meet their maker. We had all taken a turn at wheeling these pathetic vestments in barrows to the furnace. Now our wood-cutting detail set out early, equipped with tools for the job, and guarded by four Russian auxiliaries, including the big Cossack already known to us generally, but more especially to my friend Blue. This brutal guard visited our workshop one day and demanded that Blue lengthen the chain of a certain crucifix, a token which represented, had represented for a crazy moment, the value of a young man's life. It was forbidden to wear such an object – so what of that? The guard's instruction was a provocation aimed at my still unspeaking friend. In fact, a bitter rivalry already existed between these two. That was hardly surprising. At the heart of the matter were a slaughtered baby and this whole question of the girl.

Throughout the morning our party of ten felled the trees and chopped the wood before stacking the logs in neat pyramids ready for collection by a second detail later in the day. It was as we broke for lunch (lunch is really too strong a word for what passed between us) that I first felt the influence from the wooded area around us of something unspecified or unseen but nonetheless present and real. It was a kind of lure. It exerted a pull – the pull of the partisans, you might say. I could find no other explanation for this phenomenon. When I looked around, I detected nothing unusual – ten tired men rested on stones in a clearing, watched at a distance by four guards. Then I spotted it. One of their weapons had become detached from our posse of auxiliaries. This machine gun sat propped up against a rock, its muzzle pointing at the sky. Was it a ploy, a ruse, a trap laid for sport? Abruptly, one of our number, a carpenter by trade, made a dash for the weapon and bolted with it towards the trees. He was cut down from behind by a negligent burst of gunfire just before he reached the woods with their promise of refuge. In that moment I felt lost – humbled and humiliated by a young man's desperate act. Yes, *act*. What was it that so affected me? It was the idea I had that no one actually wanted to be liberated by the partisans – not really. Life was lived better inside the gates than outside them. This moral cowardice was both shameful and shaming. No one spoke of it, but all felt it – I had no doubts in that regard. It was the product of evil, the evil of the camp. Then it struck me with force – redemption lay in resistance by any means and at any price. Wasn't that the lesson of this young man's last hopeless journey? It wasn't work that would set us free. It was death. When we made to recover the carpenter's body, we were told to leave it to the partisans and their bitch queen.

That evening in the quartermaster's office I felt it strongly – a determination to move my mission, such as it existed and whatever it amounted to, forward on whatever front, or fronts, I could find. I had been summoned to receive a new design brief from the camp commandant. On this occasion I was to fashion a special item – a soft toy in the form of a koala bear – for his personal comfort and joy. He himself had no children. This latest commission was merely proof of regression towards the womb, Benjamin suggested, rolling his eyeballs disloyally.

'Do you know the man in the framed photograph behind you?' I asked him, cutting to the chase in line with my renewed focus.

'It's possible,' he said after a revealing delay, shrugging without bothering to look behind him at the shelf.

'In that case – do you also know where I can find him?' I asked, pulse quickening. 'I mean – is he still alive?'

'Maybe and maybe. Look – I don't want to lie to you. I'm done with all that. I'm here, as far as I understand it, to help you identify traitors and informants on the rebel side. That's a joke in itself, isn't it? Where are these people? Mostly dead is where. Anyway, beyond that I can't help you.'

'What do you know?' I asked. 'What have you seen?'

'Too much,' Benjamin said. 'Too much –'

We were both lost, me perhaps even more than this unhappy youth. That was how I saw the thing then. How could I be expected to know the truth about Benjamin S? By swapping sides he had sold his soul to the devil. Now he had turned, or half turned, again. Was there a way back for him? I could ask myself the same question. I was here to spot the traitors. What, then, was Benjamin? Frenchie was slightly different – he was a stooge, a plant. At all events, I could hardly denounce my key contacts. It was ludicrous. I was ridiculous. In my mind I reached out to Samuelson. What was it he once told me? *You are never alone.* Samuelson was to blame for this moral mess.

Samuelson bore ultimate responsibility for my loss of faith. Had he sent me here to choke in a sealed bunker? He must have known all along about the final solution as practised in the hills and valleys of bonny Scotland. *You are never alone.* This mantra I repeated over and over again in my head while Benjamin looked on, startled perhaps by a version of rage he saw in me. There was the picture of K– on the shelf. There was the presence of Samuelson in my head. There was the Jewish turncoat behind a desk in this room. They were all connected. We were all connected. For an instant I saw the set-up clearly. My mission had little to do with traitors or quislings. It was as I had always wanted to believe. My true mission had everything to do with locating K–. He was near me now. He was getting closer. That I would find him was a certainty, a fact. I no longer doubted it. Samuelson had known it from the word go. Hadn't he staged this whole circus? Samuelson wanted me to find K–. No – he *needed* me to render that service for him. Why? Even Benjamin saw what was happening – he saw it but he couldn't, or wouldn't, share it. Again, why? Everyone knew more than I did. Were they rooting for me, or laughing at me? They were all just waiting for the penny to drop.

That night it occurred again. Blue rolled off the mattress below mine at twelve bells and left our Nissen hut noiselessly as usual. The difference this time was as follows – I tailed him at a decent remove, both of us dodging the searchlights that wheeled about in graceful arcs from high above the central courtyard. There were a surprising number of women in the camp at any one time. They were billeted separately in a hut sited close to the kitchens in which most of them worked. Blue made directly, or as directly as the restless searchlights allowed, for this location, as I knew he would. Ruth was waiting in the still night air, her back pressed against the wall of the hut a short distance from the door. Suddenly, there was light, an abundance of

172

light, raining down from above. I saw the Cossack seize Ruth's arm. She gave out a little cry as he pulled her towards him. Seconds later they rounded the corner and were lost immediately to the dark.

BLUE SAID NOTHING OF HIS LETHAL INTENTION. He said nothing about anything at all during this critical phase of our confinement. He was struck dumb. True, he had had a terrible shock – doubtless he sought comfort where he might find it. I wasn't unduly surprised or concerned by Blue's self-imposed exile. I always knew he would regain the faculty of speech when the circumstances were right – at a time, in other words, of his own choosing. And perhaps that time had arrived. We were all of us at our usual work stations within the precious items department of the camp, awaiting the coming of this or that guard or auxiliary with a private commission, or an official request, for design and manufacture. Looking back, I might have expected to detect a quantum of tension in our hut, given what was to come. There was none. Rather, there was a good deal of silly talk, by turns passionate and insincere, about the queen of the partisans and her defining attributes or characteristics.

'Her foremost quality,' suggested Daniel, 'is mercy. It's simple – once you reach the top of the tree you can afford to be generous to the back-stabbers below you.'

'Her astonishing beauty,' offered Levi, 'is sufficient to make the rivers flow upstream and the birds give up song.'

'Don't exaggerate,' said Aaron. 'Her beauty is enough to turn a man to stone and nothing more.'

'Are you out of your tiny minds?' Cyclops asked. 'This so-called queen is a crone, a hag, with snakes for hair and hot coals for eyes.'

'What say you, Oscar?' Frenchie put in finally. 'Don't tell me she hasn't consoled you in your bunk bed at around midnight –'

As a matter of fact, the partisan queen was seldom on my mind during those dark days and nights. I was on the point of making my contribution to this harmless banter when the door of our workshop opened with more violence than was usual. It was the Cossack, of course, come to collect his cross and chain from Blue. The auxiliary took off his great coat and hung it on the back of the door. Taking up position behind our stools he started to caress Blue's cheek in a region where the stubble refused to grow.

'Do you have something special for me?' he said, bending over the shaved head, the one I had cropped with maximum tenderness only yesterday. 'I believe you have something special for me –'

Then Blue got up carefully without replying and slid the cross and chain from a pouch on the bench and circled close beside the Cossack in order to fasten chain and pendant around the thick neck from behind like a dutiful lover. Thus it was that the auxiliary's final moments in this world began with an act of devotion, and no doubt it was this unfamiliar condition that betrayed him. Out came Blue's little knife, and with one quick pass of the blade across the Cossack's throat it was done. The blood came out copiously. Who knew there was so much of it to hand? Aaron threw the coat over the Cossack's head, and for half a minute or so we six guest workers shunted the lurching man around the hut until he collapsed at last in the corner beside the smelter, the cairn of logs, and the wood-cutting tools that began there and then to suggest a route out of this unscripted mess. I cite six workers. Frenchie played no part in this murderous action, as befitted his ambiguous status within our bandit society. What can I say? Frenchie's time would come soon enough.

For a short while no one spoke. Had they discussed it with each other? Had they plotted the whole grisly deed with Blue but without Oscar? Most certainly, they had. They had left me out of the picture

174

deliberately, by consensus, in case I should prove too squeamish, or too *something*, for the deed. Now they awaited my verdict.

'Use the coat,' I said, 'to soak up the blood. Better dismember that considerable corpse *fast*, gentlemen –'

What occurred next took me by surprise. I was aware that one of us, Aaron, stood at the door, blocking it – that made sense for an obvious reason. We others were placed here and there around the interior of the hut like the offence in a basketball team. Still, no one else spoke up or spoke out. Suddenly, I saw what would take place very soon in this blood-soaked workshop. Had they discussed it with each other? Had they planned it without me in case I should prove *too something* for the game? Of course, they had. First, Frenchie made a spirited lunge at the window. Then he gave in, turned to face his fate, and drew himself up. For a moment there was silence. At this point the condemned man said an odd thing. 'Those time travellers out there –' he said. 'What are they going to think when they finally get back home?' They came at him from three directions. He went down fighting, but without otherwise making a big fuss, and for this I was proud of, and grateful to, him. In the end, the manner of his passing was not dissimilar to that of the Cossack, but Frenchie gave up the ghost much more readily than the other man.

Now the day took on a novel lease of life. We urgently needed to dispose of two bodies. I was thinking hard. I had played no active part in Frenchie's death. Having said that, I did nothing to prevent it occurring. On balance I was glad – not so much happy as relieved – that the others had acted for me, and when I considered the whole thing later I was ashamed of myself without knowing why. As you were – I knew exactly why. It was a squalid way to die for someone who had, after all, saved my life. (Point of order and information – this same someone it was who made early mention of the so-called prisoner swap, although I paid it no regard back then.) Meanwhile, there was no time to waste on idle regrets. Immediately, I set about dragging Frenchie's blood-splattered corpse away from the window area towards the corner of the workshop where the Cossack's body already lay, face to the sky, in a state of uncharacteristic repose.

'Wait up.' These two syllables heralded the unexpected return of my friend Blue to the spoken word, as far as I was aware at least. Everyone stood still and listened to him. 'What are you doing?' he went on mildly, his question framed very much for my benefit.

'It occurs to me,' I said, 'that we would be far better off without these two bodies in our midst. I was thinking in terms of a chainsaw and a wheelbarrow and an on-site incinerator I know.'

'Is that the best way forward, I wonder?' Blue said, casting his eye democratically around the hut. 'If we keep our nerve here there may be a cleverer solution, by which I mean a tidier one, available to us. After all, they think Frenchie is – sorry, *was* – one of us, don't they? So, the poor fellow had a run-in with the volatile Russian and before you could say Jack Robinson it was all up with both of them. Poetic justice, you might say. Honours even. A no-score draw –'

'Tit for tat,' Levi observed thoughtfully.

'Quid pro quo,' Aaron argued pedantically.

'An eye for an eye,' Daniel confirmed biblically.

'It couldn't have happened to two more deserving types,' Blue judged grimly, reaching down to the Cossack's body in order to rip the bloody crucifix away. 'Yours, I believe,' he said to me, thrusting the cross into my hand in much the same way Mrs Samuelson had done with the advice back then that it might one day save someone's life. Now I took stock. A lot had happened in a short space of time – more than enough to muddy the waters or queer the pitch. What did it all mean for the way we lived? 'I don't think he'll be needing it any more,' Blue said, conflating the dead man at my feet with the relic in my hand. 'Shall I shorten the chain for you, Oscar?'

He had found a new voice after a long period of self-imposed silence. There was a new mettle or metal in there, a hint of steeliness which I didn't at first recognise but which I took to be a mark of the man from now on. There would be no concession to sentiment with regard to Frenchie. That was a pity. Never mind – there was a new respect for my friend inside the hut. His solution to the problem of the twin corpses was a smart one. Was he still my friend after what had just happened here? To me there had been a subtle shift in the balance of our relationship, a realignment that pained me then and also later. Everything changes. Nothing lasts which is good. If there was a new confidence in Blue, it pleased and saddened me all at the same time. He had certainly discovered his true leaning here at the school of death. In my hurt imagination this had nothing to do with his preference for the knife, and everything to do with the girl.

That night, word came through from the carpentry boys. They had been ordered to construct a scaffold in the quadrangle at very short notice. This installation would have several steps rising up to it, and a gibbet and a trapdoor in the classical tradition. There was to be a public execution in our camp.

THEY HAD BEEN SAWING AND HAMMERING since dawn, and now the thing was up. On the northern side of the central courtyard, it rose to a commanding height above the ground – high enough, that is, to ensure a good view for all. At the same time, it was sited very deliberately at the margin of the square – it made no sense to defer the processing of our daily influx on account of this new distraction. The solitary noose, of a virgin material so outrageously fresh it hurt the eye, descended from the gallows pole in accordance with all the relevant height and weight inputs. Now the carpentry bods stepped back to admire their work, or, in the case of their anxious foreman, rehearsed the trapdoor release procedures with an understandable focus on making a success of everything. The scaffold is a primitive instrument. Nevertheless, all must be done right.

For hour after hour of the night in our smoky (we kept a stove burning at all times to discourage bed bugs) Nissen hut the talk had been of putative nooses *plural*. Our merry band was quite naturally of a single discomforting opinion – the scaffold-to-be had our name on it. There would be not just one hoop of rope swaying starkly in the breeze come morning but *several*. We thoroughly deserved it. A tooth for a tooth. Hadn't we just killed two people more or less with our bare hands? In all this there was little relief to be had from the mouths of the carpenters and cabinet makers themselves. They kept professionally mum about their brief for much of the night. When at last the word filtered through on the subject of a single noose, or a solitary execution, it failed to dampen the unpleasant speculation, at least in *my* department. Quite simply, I saw my own sweet self at the bottom of that rope, clothes soiled, eyes bulging under the hood. All is vanity, right up until the end. My companions tried to lift my spirits using an unlikely shortlist of alternative candidates, from the partisan queen to the camp commandant himself, who might just as easily be earmarked for the drop when the new day arrived. Blue, by the way, was well out of all this dawn watch conjecture. He had slipped out of our hut as usual to keep his romantic rendezvous, this time without the prospect of a burly rival in tow.

We began to gather in the courtyard immediately after eleven bells. In our group, somewhere near the middle of the assembly, I counted Blue, Daniel, Levi, Aaron, Cyclops, Benjamin and – a last-minute addition this to our number – Ruth herself. When she took

178

up position deftly between her lover and his best friend I picked up the message very clearly. This confident woman recognised she had come between us – it was unfortunate, she was saying, but that was the way things were. I could scarcely challenge her to a duel. In any case, she had the air of someone who could look after herself when the chips were down. A great shout went up in the square. I suppose I started in those bloodthirsty moments to let go of my friend Blue. Another shout went up. The hanging event had begun.

The prisoner was escorted from the northern end of the camp by a kind of guard of honour made up of the most fanatical ultras. No need to question the commitment of these baby-faced zealots – their pride in their work was apparent to the most casual observer. At this time the question began to circulate in increasingly excited whispers – would the camp commandant himself (no one seriously expected *him* to be the one to swing) grace the occasion with his rare presence? In fact, he was arriving now, conveyed from his summer residence in a sedan chair by four of his stoutest henchmen.

'Look – there he is. I told you – he approves of a good hanging every once in a while.'

'*Pour encourager les autres*, I dare say. That young man is a legend in his own lifetime.'

'I can't see him. How can you be sure it's actually him? It could be a lookalike in there – in case of attempted assassination.'

'It's him all right. Look out for the tell-tale veil covering half his face, and the black glove when he waves.'

By now the assembled necks were craning to get a better view of the prisoner. Everyone could see he was a man. But which man? Did anyone here represented know the poor fellow?

'I tell you what – I don't recognise this old codger at all. I really wouldn't know him from Adam.'

'Where on earth did they dig this duffer up? He looks half dead already. I might have to ask for my money back at this rate.'

'Hush your mouth, and show some respect for the condemned man. Don't you know it's all in the manner of the dying?'

It was Samuelson. It was Samuelson up there on the platform with his hands tied behind his back. And, yes, he did look a tad the worse for wear. To say I got a nasty shock would be to understate the case in a serious way. I pressed forward involuntarily. I needed to be closer to Samuelson. In many ways he was like a father to me. Or, at least, I had been told by his wife that he often viewed me as a son. At all events he was my mentor, my friend, and the custodian of my precious library of history books. I felt a restraining hand on my arm. Whose hand? In fact, it was Ruth who bid me stay. What subtle emotion passed between us in that moment? Up on the stage they were reading the citation now. This proclamation, which had much to do with treachery and double dealing and, yes, *books*, was read solemnly by the officer with the toothbrush moustache. They had decided that they could no longer indulge my mentor with his star status and his flagrant disregard for adversarial norms. There would be no hood for poor Samuelson – that was the real mark of his perfidy, of its extreme nature. On went the noose. There was a pause here for effect on the part of the executioner-in-chief. No one wants to blink and miss certain details. When they asked him if he had anything to say, the condemned man said he did. *Under the bridge at midnight.* That is what he said. It is all he said. When they saw he had nothing more cogent to add to this parting shot they pulled the lever below deck and Samuelson went down without a hitch.

There was a lot of disgruntled analysis of the hanged man's last utterance. What was he on about? Where was he coming from with his cryptic remark, so unsatisfying to an audience? This remark held real significance for me. I felt it strongly – although he couldn't see me in the crowd, Samuelson was speaking directly to me. Again, I felt crushed by a great burden. I stood alone in the face of these few words. What were they saying? Was this an affirmation of last resort – a signal of intent, perhaps, or a call to action? What intent, then, and which action? I began to feel faint. It was hot in the courtyard, and I had had no sleep to speak of. I was in the water with K–. I don't, as a rule, swim, but I was swimming now. This was at night, with the abandoned lighthouse up ahead. A swell developed for no reason. I had lost my companion. When I looked behind, I couldn't see the shore. Then Blue laid a hand on my shoulder and shook me as if to bring me to my senses with the sun practically overhead and the hangman's rope still creaking somewhere not too far off.

'This place isn't really for us, Oscar,' he said. 'Don't you think it's about time we came up with an exit strategy of our own?'

It is impossible to describe adequately the impact Blue's words had on me. For the first time in a long while I felt as though I was walking towards something good – the rest of my life, say. Blue saw it right away. He looked into my eyes and he got it. I gave him my best chance then. I gave him a chance, but he didn't take it. Instead, he took a step back. That was when I told myself finally that I was in love with him, and that I would always be alone from now on.

There was a postscript to the hanging affair. When I turned to confront the scaffold in the almost empty square, they were loading Samuelson's body onto a cart. Walking towards me slowly in a cloud of dust with his head bowed was Benjamin. He passed by very close, as if he didn't know me, or he couldn't see me. I saw him, however. He was weeping soundlessly, big tears falling from his soft whiskers towards his rope sandals. When I thought about this later, it made perfect sense. Everything made sense later.

ACT THREE

The Escape

In the aftermath of Samuelson's very public death I felt an emotional numbness offset by an urgent sense of responsibility. The shock I experienced over the ruthless choreography of my mentor's execution was tied up with the feeling I had that time was running out for me and my mission. The walls were, so to speak, closing in. This apprehension had its more targeted or specific components – for example, my lingering suspicion that the politics of Frenchie's demise might yet prove our undoing. (It was only a matter of time, surely, before the truth about his role as an ultras agent in the field travelled north to visit our closeted campus.) On the other hand, it was just a *feeling*. There is nothing quite like a hanging for unsettling the nerves. So it was that the idea of escape began to exert a strong influence on my outlook (and on the thoughts of my companions). I now had two imperatives competing for my dreams, alongside the tableau I envisioned on a recurring basis of my books going up in flames. I had to save my own skin, and take certain others with me on that self-interested trip. And I had to keep faith with my mission, wherever it chose to lead me, with or without Samuelson calling the shots. I still couldn't see it, or perhaps I had just forgotten it – these two priorities were one and the same thing. No matter – the penny was set to drop. The structural blueprint was about to reveal itself.

It began with speculation about a tunnel. There is always talk of digging a tunnel, isn't there? The question inevitably arises – will any such activity be detected before it has a chance to deliver on its promise? All too often, regrettably, the answer is yes. Nevertheless, there is always the tunnel phase of an escape project.

'The bastards must have done it on purpose,' Levi complained bitterly. 'They've only gone and sited the best tunnel starting points as far from the fence as possible. Take this hut, for instance –'

We were at our stations in the jewellery and metals workshop near the centre of the compound. As the days became perceptibly shorter, demand for our skills ran high. I myself was crocheting two antimacassars for the camp commandant's armchairs.

'It would take us a year to dig our way out from here,' Daniel argued despondently. 'And where would we put all the earth? We'd end up having to eat it just to get rid of it in our shit.'

'My dear Daniel,' said Aaron fondly. 'Must you always lower our discussions to a scatological level? Clean up your act, please – or it's back to the lions' den for you, bible boy.'

'Ha, ha. Say, Oscar – why don't you ask your new best buddy? He must hold a key to every hut, shed, lean-to or privy in the camp. Perhaps he can advise on a subterranean route out of here –'

'May I remind you all,' I said a little wearily, 'that Benjamin S is officially on the enemy's side in this deadly game.'

While I was happy to indulge any and all talk of a tunnel as a way of raising morale, privately I had already moved on to consider alternative options for escape. There was just one problem – these options lacked any compelling shape or form.

'But isn't that simply the nature of the beast?' Blue said after I broached the subject informally with him. 'The whole point about cheating death is that it's a difficult trick to pull off. I don't want to wax philosophical about it. We just need a plan. The key thing is to know who we can trust. We need to keep our project team as small as possible in the interests of confidentiality. The other thing, in my view, is to admit that we can't necessarily take everyone with us –'

Naturally, I was willing in all contexts to welcome suggestions from Blue. At the same time, I withheld a part of my own thinking on the possibility of an escape, great or small. What if, for example, there was only room for four on the midnight train to freedom? Or two? Or one? In my mind I had already written a list of contenders for the available tickets, if it came right down to a choice. This list grew longer or shorter from hour to hour. Then I upbraided myself for my arrogance. Who was I to preside over these outcomes? Who said anyone would want to come with me anyway? There was one thing I could count on, I knew, in the ebb and flow of these vagaries – Blue would have his own manifest of escapees. How many places, I wondered, were available on his midnight train?

It was as these early inklings of a plan, or a half plan, for escape first presented themselves to me that things took a political turn for the worse. With hindsight it may be possible to see this development as a bonus – it certainly had the effect of bringing matters to a head. When I delivered my soft furnishings for the camp commandant to the quartermaster's office, Benjamin gave me the news. Word was out – they would begin liquidating the current complement of guest workers within days, replacing these with a new cohort drawn from the regular influx to our compound. It was of little comfort that this changing of the guard was a routine procedural tactic intended to control the spread of information, or disinformation, about the true nature of the camp's business.

'Remember I exist to help you deliver your mission,' Benjamin said with a renewed focus, no doubt, on his own agency in the face of diminished operational parameters. Was it not the case that he answered, directly or indirectly, to Samuelson in this context? And now Samuelson was no more.

'In order to fulfil my mission,' I said, 'it will first be necessary to stay alive.'

'Then I am here to help you in that regard too.'

'You'll forgive me when I tell you that my capacity for trusting someone – I mean anyone – has come under pressure in a difficult season. And a man who has turned once, or twice, can turn again.'

'Clever Oscar – you think you're a bit special, don't you? What do you really know of my beliefs and my motives? Can you see into another man's soul? How do you know I didn't go over to the ultras expressly to destroy them, or at least to attack them, from within?'

Was I wrong to provoke this young man? More and more now I had a sense that I wouldn't be able to do what I had to do without him. With the warning that our ranks would soon be culled came a fresh focus on mortality. Everything was, quite literally, a matter of life and death from this moment onwards. And Benjamin was right. Who was I to denounce his shifting allegiances, given my own track record in the survival stakes? We were all just playing a part. In this psychodrama the surface detail was as telling as what lurked below. When Frenchie shot my cat he was simply keeping up appearances. When they tortured me at the house of arraignment they were just keeping up appearances. As Blue said – it was all about trust, now more than ever. And I had to trust Benjamin. 'Under the bridge at midnight –' I said to him. 'Do those words mean anything to you?'

'To me they have a conclusive poetry, but also an ambiguous quality, about them. They denote jeopardy and opportunity both.'

'That isn't exactly what I was getting at,' I said. What if I was mistaken? What if these five words had no scope or reach beyond what was obvious? Could it be that they had no ulterior resonance over and above what you chose to allow them? Their significance resided solely in the fact or the possibility of their recognition by the initiated, be it in summer or winter. Was that all? There had to be more to it, didn't there? It was as if Benjamin read my thoughts.

'What are words anyway,' he said, 'if not the means by which one man might find another?'

'How long have we got?' I asked. 'Until, I mean, they march us off to the gas chambers –'

'I can't be sure,' Benjamin said. 'A few days? A few weeks? It's all done quickly and quietly, as you would expect. First there must take place what we affectionately call the prisoner swap.'

'And what prisoner swap might that be?' I asked with a good deal of native curiosity.

'Some of your number could be exchanged at the gates for our people held by the partisans in the forest. Three in, three out. Two in, two out. Et cetera, et cetera. And the moon should be full.'

'Oh,' I said, thinking hard with the image of Frenchie's corpse before me. Hadn't he once told me? Hadn't Frenchie tipped me off about the prisoner swap once upon a time while he still breathed? 'Why didn't someone mention this fascinating ritual earlier?'

'If you want my help, Oscar, you must ask for it. You want to live, don't you? Ask and you shall receive. And now I must offer you further comfort. The camp commandant is exceedingly taken with your needlework. So taken is he that he invites you to visit him in his private quarters in order to receive his thanks personally.'

Now it began. It was what I had been waiting for. 'Tell him,' I said, 'I accept his kind invitation. I enjoy wine and have no allergies. Oh, yes, and do me a small favour, would you, Benjamin? Get me on tomorrow's wood-cutting detail without fail.'

Ask and you shall receive. That night I said these words over and over again to myself as I waited anxiously to catch a glimpse of the moon. My rapidly developing lunar obsession – it was much more than a side issue designed to distract from my impending audience with the camp commandant. It was actually a dialogue with death. As for that special audience – I set it to one side in a compartment labelled *destiny*. When the moon poked its head out finally, I could see it was virtually full. What type of moon was it? Was it noble or base, blessed or benighted? Some moons are harder to gauge than others – try it yourself if you don't believe me. Was this one waxing or waning, for example? The answer came soon enough.

I TRIED NOT TO THINK ABOUT A FULL MOON. Instead, I focused on the so-called prisoner swap and its implications for my fledgling plan. Really, this had the potential to change everything. The entire notion of a solemn exchange of personnel at the gates to the citadel chimed one hundred per cent with my best instincts in the matter. I had considered and then discarded the idea of a bloody shoot-out with the auxiliaries. After we raided the armoury, enabled by a key supplied by our inside contact, we would fast develop the weaponry skills needed to eliminate the most fanatical guards before vaulting the perimeter fence using a great many ladders fashioned in short order by our friends in the forest. When I say a great many ladders, I point to the essence of the challenge. The problem was statistical. Guest worker numbers, although meaningful, were insufficient to overwhelm the forces on the ground. At the same time, there were far too many of us to undertake a traditional prisoner exchange as Benjamin had described it. Two in, two out, he had said. Three in, three out. Et cetera, et cetera. How could I manage these numerical infelicities in line with my nobler intentions? What was it Blue said?

The other thing, in my view, is to admit that we can't necessarily take everyone with us. How right my friend was. I resolved there and then to share my prisoner swap knowledge with no one, not even Blue. Especially not Blue. This injunction was a matter of practical logic as much as personal loyalty. Whereas at one time I would have regarded Blue's outlook and instincts as being squarely in line with my own, now I wasn't so sure. Love is jealous and blind. It was nobody's fault, but it mattered. In short, there was only room for one set of prejudices when it came to the delicate affair in train – my own.

With me in the wood-cutting detail that morning was Cyclops. This gentle giant had always been my favourite among the worker colleagues I had come to know over the past weeks and months. I understood nothing of his background, and he understood nothing of mine. Once when he gripped my fingers and offered to read my palm and I pulled my hand away, he told me not to worry. I would live long, he said – too long, maybe, if I could imagine such a thing. It was as the fascists intended – we two existed in, and lived for, the present only. That present was about to blow up in our faces. Yet as our party trudged in single file through the woods, connected by a looping chain and flanked by guards bearing weapons and tools, there was no tell-tale allusion to what the big gypsy directly behind me was planning. There was the usual singing and banter. We sang the old songs, the songs of our fathers. In this the guards indulged us respectfully as was normal during these forest forays, themselves joining in the odd chorus picked up over time. In between songs we speculated humorously on the eccentric ways of the partisans. The goons loved this childish horseplay.

'Fancy a shot at the flying trapeze, boyo? Step on one of their camouflaged nooses and the next thing is you'll be catapulted into the trees, never to be seen again.'

'Ready for a sojourn down under, mate? Tread on one of their cunningly concealed trapdoors and the chances are you've bought a one-way ticket to New Queensland –'

It was as I had hoped. Today's tree felling zone was once again located to the south of the camp. At all times during our expedition I was alert to the possibility of an underground railway that carried the dead bodies away from the gas chambers. There had to be some mechanism for managing this endless traffic discreetly and reliably, day in, day out. As the clock ran down on my mission and my life, I became increasingly exercised by the idea of the phantom railway as a means of escape. Was I going mad? Had I already taken leave of my senses? Very possibly – the veil of impracticality cloaking my deliberations was like a miasma, a mist. I couldn't discern the path ahead. Then, unexpectedly, my patience was rewarded. It began as an aerial hum, growing louder and getting closer. Soon the sound shifted underground, where it belonged. I judged it a cross between a rumble and a clatter, suitably muffled, that persisted for roughly a minute before gradually falling off. In our forest clearing, no one spoke. None of us *knew* – that is, we couldn't be certain. Even so, it was understood or accepted between us. We stood still with heads bowed, guards and guest workers all, as if to mark the moment of interment at the grave of a neighbour's child. Now the chains came off, and we set forth with our tools, fanning out in a circle with the guards back-to-back at its centre.

'My dear Oscar,' Cyclops began. 'You must prepare yourself for a shock.' He walked beside me at the regulation distance with a chainsaw in his arms. 'The truth is they are going to kill us soon. I mean me and you and our fellow guest workers.' Although he was talking to me, Cyclops wasn't looking at me. Each time he spoke he hesitated briefly before proceeding so that the meaning of his words might carry. His grace and courtesy in this affected me a great deal. 'Please don't concern yourself unduly, Oscar,' he continued calmly. 'We will escape, me and you, in a short time from now. Yes, we will be among the partisans at long last, living in the woods on nuts and berries. Don't say anything –'

'My good friend –' I said. I had to. 'How do you know they're going to kill us?'

'I know a girl in the kitchens. She is intimate with one of their officers. She told me.'

'When, Cyclops?' I asked, not looking at him. 'When are they planning to do this?'

'Tomorrow, or the day after. When the moon is full. It doesn't matter, Oscar. Soon we will be free. First, I shall create a diversion here in the forest. You will know when the time has come.'

Things happened pretty quickly after that. Cyclops attacked a good-sized tree with his chainsaw, and within a few seconds the old trunk began to lean. At the same time there was the sound of wood letting go of wood. Then Cyclops did a strange thing. He lay down on the forest floor in the path of the falling tree and waited for it to land on him. Immediately, he was surrounded by guards and guest workers. 'Now, Oscar, now –' he shouted. I couldn't do it. 'No, my friend –' I said. 'I'd much rather stay here with you.' In fact, it was true. It was the whole truth. (I see what you're thinking. You think I had to stay, or I wanted to stay, in order to deliver my mission. I know what you're saying. What kind of hero would I be when the moon was full if I'd already exited the scene, alone, a fugitive from danger?) 'Run, Oscar, run –' Then Cyclops reached out and seized the saw that was still active at low level beside him and brought the moving parts up to his own throat. That was how the tale ended for the gypsy. If he was going to perish anyway, he wanted his death to count for something, which it surely did. I had to wipe my friend's blood from my face, but I didn't mind. After the episode ended, we learned that one of our guards was unaccountably absent. One of the goons was missing, spirited away, evidently, by forest forces.

At the shower block beside the barracks at the northern end of the camp they gave me a towel, a square of soap, and clean clothes. I got to thinking I myself had probably fashioned these garments – how simple they seemed to me and how pleasing. This was towards evening, when the pace of life, or indeed *death*, in our camp slowed sufficiently to allow the impression, false and fleeting, of a world at peace with itself. As for the brown slab of soap – it had the effect of searing my hand as I held it. There was a limitless quantity of these soap slabs in the storerooms I visited from day to day, armed with Benjamin's keys. When I challenged him over the provenance of the odourless blocks, he looked me straight in the eye and said *don't ask*. That afternoon the water from the shower was wonderfully cool on my skin. I bowed my head below the meagre current and let it rinse from my hair and beard the last traces of my brave friend Cyclops. It was to his memory I dedicated these precious minutes of physical pleasure as I counted down slowly from a hundred inside my head. Then it was time to address the matter at hand. As my meeting with the camp commandant drew fatefully near, it seemed my whole life – everything I had ever said or done or thought or dreamed – had led me to this moment of truth. He was waiting for me now behind the veil. What facial disfigurement did it hide, this eloquent wisp of fabric? And the ubiquitous black gloves – what cruel story did they conceal from the prying eyes of the world? The biggest question of all I saved until last. Would I know him? Would I know my beloved K–? Would I recognise the monster he had become, and would I actually want to? As I rubbed myself over and over again with soap in the faltering stream, I had the idea I was washing my body in the tears of a thousand orphaned children.

On the veranda that fronted the bungalow the massive hound rose up attentively, eyed me sadly, then sank back down again with a clinking of its chain. As I approached the door I had the uncanny impression I was entering an enchanted wood at sunset – the sound of birdsong leaking from within was hallucinatory. When the door opened automatically, as if in answer to a code or command, it was as I had imagined – the interior was criss-crossed by budgerigars of yellow, green and blue. As the door swung shut behind me – again, this seemed to happen in response to a silent instruction – the birds settled as one on the pelmets above the windows on two sides of the room. In a recess on my left hung an artwork depicting the ruined lighthouse already known to my subconscious mind. Before me was a curtain of muslin, or similar, that descended from the rafters and spanned much of the breadth of the space behind a table arranged with a lone chair and a collection of books. There were books here. These slim volumes were more remarkable to me than any number of exotic birds. In that moment I recognised many of the works on the table. That was when I knew I had come home.

'Welcome, Oscar – welcome home.' The disembodied voice, alien to me and familiar, emanated from behind the curtain. 'How long have I practised these few words, so simple and improbable? And now we are together again at last.' There was a kind of lisp I didn't recognise – it gave to the most basic utterance the whispered quality of a prayer or a confession. 'Together, Oscar, and yet apart. Please forgive these curtained arrangements, which I insist on today if only to spare your feelings. The truth is my outward appearance is subtly altered since you last saw me. For these modifications I am indebted to the house of arraignment, of course. Are we not all of us, spiritually if not physically, in its debt?' There was only the voice and the silhouette thrown by the lamp towards the curtain. Nothing stirred anywhere. Neither bird nor beast made the slightest sound. 'Come closer, Oscar. Come closer so that I can see you better. My eyesight is not what it used to be. Now my dear books are strangers to me. You recognise these forbidden works, don't you? Naturally, you do. Sit down, won't you? Sit down and read to me, please. Is it too much to ask? I mean for the sake of old times, or in memory of what we once shared?'

For more than an hour I read for K– from his favourite works by Byron and Shelley, Rimbaud and Verlaine. Each time I stopped or stumbled he asked me to go on until, finally, I got up and backed away from the table in the fading light and waited for him to judge me. For a moment I imagined he was crying dry tears of sorrow or joy. Then I dismissed this notion – the man behind the cheesecloth curtain wasn't, had never been, the crying kind.

'Thank you, Oscar,' he said at last. 'You read beautifully, just as you do everything else in life. No – don't try to protest. Don't say anything, please. There is very little time left. You realise that, don't you? Tomorrow, the moon will be full. Your mission will end, as it must. You know what to do, don't you? You do? Then I am happy. You know I depend on you, friend. There can be no mistake about this. Go now, please. Until tomorrow, sweet dreams –'

Sweet dreams, indeed – that was a bitter and unlikely prospect. On the veranda beside the rocking chair the big German Shepherd approached me, licked my fingers, and whined mournfully. Above, the shooting stars were once again general in the late summer sky. In a silence local to these northernmost reaches of the compound I heard the lugubrious tolling of the camp's bell – it seemed to come from great distance, crossing prairies and oceans on its way to the

193

present. Behind me, just beyond the perimeter fence, the partisans were setting their little fires in the forest. In my hand was a volume of verse by Keats, modest in heft, and precious to me always. When hearts fail, salvation lies in things.

THE LAST DAY DAWNED COOL AND CLEAR. As the sun scraped the tops of the trees beyond the eastern limit of the camp it set out for the final time its dazzling vision of freedom through death. By then I was already steering a course towards Benjamin, summoned early by a chain of messages that passed ever more laconically from hut to slumbering hut. As I made my way hurriedly along the lanes and alleys so familiar to me I had the sensation I was walking these cruel byways for the first time. I mean – I saw with new eyes. In the long shadows between the cabins and lean-tos I thought I glimpsed the smiling faces of the ones who had perished here, the young and the old, forsaken by man, abandoned by God.

Benjamin was waiting for me in the quartermaster's cubbyhole as usual. He wasn't sitting at his desk this time – he paced from one wall to the other behind the door with a typed memorandum in his hand. 'It happens tonight,' he told me straight away. 'The prisoner swap – it starts tonight at eight bells.'

It was decided. The fuse had been lit. The remaining events – would they unfold according to the script I had carried in my head for what seemed more like days or weeks than hours? 'How many?' I asked Benjamin. It was a simple enough question. On the answer depended everything.

'Three –' he said. 'Three in, three out – just like I told you.'

'Which three?' I asked. 'I mean which three guest workers?'

'It's your show, Oscar. It's your heaven, your hell. You make the moves here now. Call it destiny. Or irony. Call it anything you

194

want. Normally, I would choose who lives and who doesn't. We all have our favourites, don't we?'

'Then let it be so,' I said. I had always known the decision or the choice would be laid at my door. I had always accepted it would come down to the numbers. It would have been just two, wouldn't it, without the unexpected attentions of my late gypsy friend? When Cyclops created his chainsaw diversion mere hours ago, he altered the maths. Now the partisans had a third prisoner to trade.

'Get your people ready shortly before the deadline,' Benjamin said. 'The identity of the three candidates remains unknown to the rest of the camp until the last moment. I can help you with all that. I'm sure you appreciate the need for discretion. We don't want an ill-tempered riot to spoil the party, do we? One more thing, Oscar. The three men – men and women if it comes to that – will be roped together at the neck an arm's length apart. Don't ask why. There is comfort, it strikes me, in tradition. The rest is darkness –'

'Ritual cannot save us,' I said. 'Yet in the absence of true faith, we still cleave to the trappings of belief, don't we?' Three in, three out – so be it. But which three would march through the gates into the arms of the partisans? If I told you I didn't actually know, would you take my word for it? There was one more item on my personal agenda that morning in the quartermaster's den. It was a long shot – I knew that, of course. At the same time it had to it a fitness or an inevitability. What I had in mind – quite simply, it was a last throw of the dice. How else would I get the numbers to add up? 'Tell me, Benjamin –' I said. 'What befalls the bodies from the gas chambers at the end of the long day? Are they, perhaps, helped on their way towards the consoling flames by a mechanical intervention?'

It was hotter, and the sun was laughing at me from the sky. My next appointment was with Blue. I discovered him sitting on a stool, peeling potatoes, outside the kitchen block where he spent much of his time now in order to be with Ruth. I hadn't rehearsed what to say to Blue. Wasn't he my trusted lieutenant in everything? Or was that marvellous phase gone forever? I still respected Blue too much to take him, or anything about him, for granted. In fact, I had the strong conviction I would need his help before the day was through. No, not just his help – his validation and approval. Doubtless I had always needed, or wanted, these things from my friend.

'We go tonight,' I began instinctively, my voice low, crouching beside Blue with my back against the wooden wall. It didn't matter that this confident assessment was not yet more than an aspiration. I believed it. Or, rather, I believed *in* it – I had to. With the support, in various key areas, of my principal partners I would most certainly make it work. Yes, I would make the numbers add up.

'We?' Blue said, without pausing in his task. 'To whom are you referring there, Oscar?'

Did he know they were about to start terminating us? I hadn't discussed this with Blue. Even so, I felt sure he suspected something – he had a boundless affinity for survival. Hadn't Cyclops indicated his own insights came from these very kitchens? In all of this I was obliged to strike a nice balance. If our imminent executions were to become common knowledge, it would inevitably spark an ill-fated insurrection in the camp. Would that be helpful to the cause of our escape, of our necessarily limited escape? Had Blue also seen these salient factors in play? Had he too wrestled with the idea of the few versus the many? Actually, it didn't matter. Benjamin was right – it was my show now. I had my blueprint for escape. It involved a very few individuals only. You think me callous? I ask you in good faith – what would you have done in my shoes? 'When I say we,' I told Blue, 'I mean you and me, of course. You and me and one other.'

'One other?' Blue said. 'I presume you refer there to tonight's prisoner swap of three.'

'You know about that?' I asked needlessly. It was one thing to know about the prisoner exchange – it was quite another to have a grasp of the arithmetic. Not for the first time, I paid silent tribute to my resourceful friend. What I waited for above all was his insistence on including Ruth in our human quotient.

'There's something you should know,' he said, as if he read my thoughts. 'Ruth is pregnant.' Here, he lobbed a potato into the pail of water between his feet and waited for his words to sink in. 'Soon the baby will start to show,' he added meaningfully. 'It follows that Ruth must depart the camp. In order to guarantee this, I am willing – no, happy – to sacrifice my place tonight.' Neither of us spoke for a while. I had a vision of the Cossack seizing Ruth and making off with her at dead of night in this exact location. Then Blue took up again. 'I know what you're thinking, Oscar, and it doesn't matter to me. It doesn't matter whether or not the baby is mine.'

The sun monitored us religiously. I had never felt closer to my friend than I did then. I said nothing of the Cossack and what I had seen that night. There was no call for this. 'It will be as you choose,' I told Blue, getting up and stepping into the glare. 'You said trust was everything. Can I count on you tonight?'

Then Blue looked up at me, eyes shining, from his narrow strip of shade. 'Have you forgotten you once saved my life?' he enquired passionately. 'I'll do whatever you ask me to. There has never been any argument about this. You have only to say the word. Don't you know that by now?'

That afternoon we five – Levi, Aaron, Daniel, Blue and myself – worked as usual at our stations. I was able, in spite of everything, to finish off a pair of silk pyjamas commissioned days earlier by my regular sponsor. Little was said in our cabin. At six bells I gave my companions their instructions, then traipsed north wearing the red armband that conferred immunity from prosecution in the camp. He was already waiting for me behind the cheesecloth curtain with the colourful birds swooping all around him. I came fully prepared for what I had to do. Soon it would be over, for K— and for me. In the shower I prayed for a successful outcome to the evening's work. I had never prayed before – not like that. I didn't even know who I was praying to. Nevertheless, the words were a comfort to me. As I rinsed off the shameful soap, I had the idea I was washing from my ignoble body all the sins of the world.

Beside the rocking chair on the veranda outside the bungalow the big hound raised its head in greeting. There was something new – two unmarked flagons sat on the decking together with a box of matches, their collective import immediately plain. Right away, my pulse quickened. As I closed the front door behind me the swooping birds took up position on the pelmets as before. In front of me was the thin drape and the table arranged with chair and books. For an hour I read to K— from the volumes he loved. Every now and again he gave a little cry of wonder or a murmur of approval, occasionally asking me to repeat a favourite couplet or stanza. Faster, he would say. No – slower. Or louder. Or softer. And I was happy to deliver these small favours to K— as our time together ran down. At last, I set aside the final volume. In my hand was the protective canister which housed the tiny pill once gifted me with a feverish speech by Mrs Samuelson in the doorway of a southern apartment. I popped the tablet into my mouth, and rose from the table.

He lifted the drape and glided towards me. As he drew nearer, he stripped the gloves from his hands, discarding these dark sheaths on the table, and raised the veil at his face. He had no lips as such

– that was the thing. The lips were missing, as were the tips of the fingers, shorn off at the level of the first joint.

'Thank you again, Oscar,' he said with his peculiar lisp. 'Now I am content, and ready for the last act. Two more things I ask you to do for me, please. On the table behind me is a key – a key to the dog's chain. Take care of No-Name for me, won't you, friend? Pets are forbidden – we know that. But you will find a way. There are two flagons of gasoline on the veranda outside. Use them wisely and well, please.' Here, he licked his lips, or what was left of them. 'Now it is time,' he told me. 'Kiss me, Oscar – yes, a kiss before dying.' He took one last step towards me. I was thinking about Samuelson and the accursed brief he had given me, which was to liquidate a rogue operative once dear to my heart. Only I could come close enough for such a delicate assignment. It was a mission, or an outcome, for which Samuelson had paid with his life. Soon the story would end, and K– would get what he most wanted, which was to be released from an idea of himself and what he had become. As I kissed my friend goodbye, I planted the tablet inside his mouth and withdrew. He had the option then of spitting the thing out, but he didn't take it up. I watched him bite on the capsule and shudder. A great sigh of peace issued from deep inside him. Then his eyeballs rolled up. Within a few seconds he was on the floor at my feet with the pink froth at his teeth and the red wine leaking from his ears. I snatched the key from the table and backed away from the scene. At the same time, I heard the first chants from far off.

The ceremonial corridor ran from the great gates towards the main quadrangle of the camp. On either side of the road the goons faced those assembled north and south, these armed guards strung out in long lines with their backs to each other. Every lamp was lit. From the control towers on either side of the gates the searchlights probed the nearest trees for evidence of the partisans. A shout went up. Roped together at the neck, Levi, Daniel and Aaron began the trek from square to perimeter fence. Now the chants started over. *Death or freedom! Freedom or death!* There was even a homage here and there to the mythical mother of the forest. *Long live the queen! May the queen live!* I had beside me Blue and Ruth. Soon we were joined by Benjamin S, his prisoner exchange duties discharged. As the three men bound for freedom drew level with us, I felt an emotion unlike anything I had experienced in the camp. Then I turned to Blue and gave him the key and the red armband.

'Leave the door open,' I told him. 'That way the birds will have a chance to escape. Use the petrol unreservedly, my friend, but be sure the dog is safely with you before you strike the match.'

Now a great silence reigned. As the big gates swung open, the full moon deigned to appear finally in line with local custom. Then the partisans stepped forward from the trees to form their corridor of engagement, young men mostly, of filthy overall appearance and with mud-daubed faces. A new shout went up. Bound together neck and foot, the trio of captive goons hobbled, squinting, towards the lights, the gates, and their prisoner swap counterparts. Very soon now my three companions would walk, or limp, free. I had to stay long enough to be certain. I had to make sure it really happened.

We made directly for the huddle of huts and sheds at the heart of the compound, Ruth following Benjamin, with me bringing up the rear. No one stopped or challenged us – weren't we escorted by the camp's chief fixer? Less than three minutes later we were at the palisade that protected the killing quarter. No lights burned here – Benjamin had made sure of that. As we approached the outer doors of the gas chambers, we heard the camp's bell toll furiously. Behind us to the north, sparks from the fire climbed high into the sky. Inside the chambers there was literally nothing to see. Apparently, this was a location where nothing ever occurred. There were two rail tracks, one for goods out, and one for goods in. In practice, of course, there were no goods in – just empty wagons returning from the fire. Ruth curled up in the second carriage from the buffers, under instruction from Benjamin. He and I would take the first, as in nearest, wagon. At length we heard the excited barking of the dog. No-Name would ride with Blue and Ruth in the van of our convoy. There was only one switch to trip, and Benjamin tripped it, his ring of keys jangling anxiously. Immediately, we were on our way. I don't think anyone spoke after that. What was there to discuss? At the same time, it was hard not to dwell on it – at any moment our absence, or the means of our exit, might be discovered. From second to second I expected our transport to grind sickeningly to a halt before going into reverse. It didn't happen that way – I don't know why. I carried my book of poems inside my shirt, and I had my cross around my neck. For an hour there was only a sticky dew that dripped, squeezed out against all odds, from the forest floor above, plus a profound darkness.

THEY TOOK US TO THEIR HEADQUARTERS, or one of their larger enclaves, which was located who knows where in the middle of the forest. I didn't ask them. We didn't ask. They seemed to make their way through the woods under the direction of an instinctual radar, a navigational resource available to the few. Our job was simply to keep up with them, the big dog shadowing us faithfully from beside Blue. This was after they subjected our renegade wagons to benign ambush in the area of the forest where the railway rose up gradually from below during its passage to a sunlit sea. Our hurtling progress was first slowed and then stopped by a series of improvised buffers made of branches and lesser boughs. How did they know we were coming? We didn't ask. In a woodland world they were masters of all they surveyed or sanctioned. In the realm of moss and bark there was nothing they didn't perceive or apprehend. As we entered their settlement at first light, the overnight coals glowing in one hundred braziers at high and low level around us, I had the impression I was either dreaming or dead.

We slept for a whole day. I refer here to Benjamin, Blue, Ruth and myself. The dog called No-Name pined for its new master from the forest floor below. When we rose finally we found it was true – this really was a city in the trees. In all directions a lattice of timber structures lay claim to the interior, these outposts connected to each other by rope bridges and accessed via a modular system of ladders and ramps. They had prepared a feast in our honour. There were nuts and berries, of course, plus game and a punch. There was also a lavish garland of flowers, which I took to be a type of tribute. This hoop of infinite regard was presented to Benjamin by a child of the partisans. He was a hero to them, it seemed – a figure universally loved and respected. I was about to find out why.

At dusk they lit a great many fires and torches all around the settlement, and the atmosphere was one of mounting excitement. By then the word was out – the partisan queen herself would join our little celebration. This was a shock, of course. But there were a couple of other surprises awaiting my attention as the smoke from the fires formed a blue haze in the sky above the camp. This smoke, by the way, had a characteristic aroma. It left a metallic taste in the mouth and had an enervating quality, so that I began to suspect I was under the influence of some mild narcotic.

At first, I heard singing. This singing grew steadily louder until, finally, the eagerly anticipated guests entered the clearing to terrific fanfare. There was a banging of drums and a blaring of pipes at this time. Heading up the procession of new arrivals were Levi, Aaron and Daniel, one behind the other and each garlanded with flowers. Suddenly she was with us, the mythical mother of the forest. As she lurched towards our astonished group of refugees, her hair setting forth to all points of the compass, Mrs Samuelson reached out with both arms towards Benjamin. Was it a gesture of welcome or a plea for his love? Then I understood what was happening. I saw the tears fall from his face in the aftermath of a hanging. Those tears he shed for his father, whose body they loaded onto a cart. Benjamin S was a true Samuelson. Now he was reunited with his famous mother.

'Were you there?' she asked him. 'Did you witness it?'

'Yes,' he told her. 'I saw everything, as he would have wanted.'

'I'm glad,' she said. 'I'm glad one of us was there at the end.'

I remember little about our foraged supper that night. As I say, it is possible my senses were the target of some obscure influence to which the rest of the world was immune. The next morning I woke up refreshed and ready to leave the camp. No packing was needed. I had my book in my hand.

'Where will you go?' Mrs Samuelson asked me as I prepared to say my farewells.

'To the sea,' I said. 'I haven't seen nearly enough of the sea, and it is not so far away now.'

'Do you know how to get there?' she asked urgently.

'No,' I told her. 'But I plan to find out.' Then I put my question to her. 'Your crucifix –' I said, bringing the intrepid talisman into the light. 'Will you take it back from me now?'

'Not now,' she whispered with her extraordinary capacity for passion. 'Not yet –' The spasms which rocked her body periodically were very much on display. Doubtless their incidence and intensity were a product of her state of mind at any moment. The more she felt, the more she shook. Abruptly, I drew near to her in a flashback. This was in another lifetime. I asked her why she was so often away from home, and she was discreetly metaphorical in reply. Where is home? I am taking time out, she told me, to travel.

When I said goodbye to my companions there was a good deal of raw emotion in the air around us. Levi cried, Daniel prayed, and Aaron bowed his head as though he couldn't bear to look at me. I am bound to say the dog licked my fingers disconsolately. Benjamin pumped my hand and hugged me like a brother. As for Ruth and Blue – they kissed me solemnly in turn and told me they loved me, and this was something special to me, with more to come. We had gathered in the main clearing at about midday with the sun shining straight down from a cloudless sky.

'Our baby is also your baby,' Ruth told me with her hand on her stomach where the bump was starting to show. 'This baby will save us all from yesterday, today and tomorrow. And perhaps even from the idea of death itself –'

'It's going to be a boy,' Blue added with a note of something like pride in his voice.

'Oh?' I said interestedly. 'How do you know? I mean – how can you be certain of that?'

'The big gypsy told me,' Ruth said, smiling and remembering. 'Cyclops read my palm. Actually, he read it more than once. I asked him to do it several times because I wanted to be sure.'

'It's a boy,' Blue confirmed gravely. 'And guess what? This boy will be christened Oscar. There is no other name we could choose or want for our son.'

Can you imagine how difficult it was to leave these hospitable glades? If I stayed here for just one more day, I told myself, I might never go. From the edge of the clearing I looked back with a heavy heart. They were all watching me. They were watching me, hands raised, as if to acknowledge they would never set eyes on me again. Then her voice, strong and clear in the hush, bolstered my will. She had her faith and her reasons. She was a myth, a legend. She would take time out, she was telling me, to travel.

'Wait up, please,' she called out from somewhere in the trees. 'I'm coming with you. I will show you the way.'

BEHIND US WAS THE OLD CAPITAL. In front stretched the ancient kingdom of Fife. Below us, the two fallen bridges straddled the river in shattered segments, half in and half out of the water, their rusty girders the preserve now of rats and other small mammals feasting on sewage and snagged corpses. Was there indeed a giant pipeline transporting bodies to the sea? Hadn't my companions of yesterday speculated fancifully on just such a possibility? In the air above the river was the most delicate smir – a drizzle so fine it could be felt but not seen. The sky was very low – a child could have reached up and touched it. In the east, where the river spread its arms wide to greet the sea, we saw an odd thing. Had a plane come down too steeply for its own good? Was a cruise ship drowning out there somewhere, holed below the water line and listing hard? Impossible to say. The flotilla of life jackets, inflated but unmanned, drifted towards the coast in tight formation, blood orange, an epiphany.

'What will you do now?' I asked her. Here at slight altitude the suggestion of a breeze reached us from the sea – it wreaked minor havoc on her intelligent hair. 'I mean without him?'

'I don't know,' she said. 'Resist better, I imagine. No doubt he would expect nothing less –'

Resist better? What could she mean by that? I was thinking of his futile death. All was futility. In my mind's eye I saw the partisans

205

at work by night – they were digging up the railway tracks that led to and from the liquidation zone. Then I saw the goons – they were laying the same tracks down again just after dawn. I had the image in my head of his bloated body floating far out at sea, way beyond the reach of the eternal pipeline. I was thinking about his battle cry, his rallying cry, and what it might mean for me, or for her, or for those of us who still cared. 'Does it have any special significance?' I asked her in a fierce whisper. 'Under the bridge at midnight?'

'What,' she asked, 'would you like it to mean? During the first insurrection they paraded the bodies of the disappeared under the bridges along the Thames. At midnight the mothers came by boat to identify the dead and to cut them down. Does such a description satisfy you, Oscar? Is it enough? When the apocalypse comes you'll find me under the bridge at midnight. Let fire rain down all around us – the great viaduct of broken bodies offers shelter from the storm. What else can I tell you? *Under the bridge at midnight.* These five words mean nothing and everything. They are the proof of our story. We must keep saying them, Oscar. We must insist on them in the face of a slaughter. First, they will try to wipe us out. Then they will deny it. Given enough time, the lie becomes truth. Soon the ideal notion, or the preferred idea, takes hold in the minds of the living – it never happened at all. Do you see where this is going? At a certain point we don't exist. The waters close over us. We no longer *matter* in any sense. Our destruction is total, our ignominy complete –'

A lone gull passed overhead. I was thinking about my own life, of its negligible value in the midst of so much death. I was nothing. My life meant nothing. Then she took my hand as if to comfort or console me. She herself didn't hurt or grieve – she was too far gone for that. Yes, it was fitting and proper to fight for every last life. Yes, it was right to argue for your own most of all. How else would the fascists be sent packing and the totalitarian hordes be put to flight? It was getting dark. It was getting dark earlier and earlier these days. Soon the chestnuts would begin falling in the sacred forests of the night. 'Is there an abandoned lighthouse in this part of the world?' I asked her at last.

'There are many,' she said. 'They exist always just out of sight. Why? Did you dream of one?'

'In a manner of speaking,' I said. 'Funny – I saw a painting of it on the wall of his bungalow.'

'Some things cannot be explained,' she said. 'It must be proof of your strong feeling for him.'

'I have his book,' I said. 'The painting is no more, but I have his volume of poems by Keats.'

'Ah, Keats,' she said. 'Did you know that was his name? K for Keats. That's what it stood for. He once begged me not to tell you. He said he was unworthy of such a name. I told him he was wrong.'

'No –' I said. 'I didn't know. But I'm not surprised. How little we understand each other really –'

'The day is almost done,' she noted elegiacally. 'What will you do, Oscar? Will you go home?'

'Where is that?' I asked her. 'You and I – we have no home. We are prisoners of our freedom.'

'Home, my dear boy,' she retorted somewhat sternly, 'is where your books are.'

'Ah, yes, my books –' I said. 'My books will be delinquent ashes by now.'

'In that case,' she said, 'you must start a new collection, a new library, beginning with a volume of verses snatched from the fire.'

The light was disappearing rapidly on the western flank of the world. We two stood hand in hand on the bluff above the choking river. In the east, the sky was welded darkly to the sea. 'Over there!' she exclaimed, pointing. Then I saw it – a lamp flashing dimly every few seconds from the depths of the murk. 'Did you see?' she said, laughing. 'It appears the lighthouse is not yet abandoned.' As time dissolved, or fell off, I waited for her to invoke a well-known crucifix in noble metals with lustrous gems attached. She didn't mention it, and neither did I. I still wear that fabulous cross today.

This imperfect and inadequate tale I dedicate to the men, women and children who perished in the Nazi death camps of Europe between 1940 and 1945, and to those who survived.
Barry Stewart Hunter, London, March 2023.

Ingram Content Group UK Ltd.
Milton Keynes UK
UKHW042048080323
418270UK00004B/42